MY M[...]
IS A
ROCK STAR

MW00938663

**LAURA DREW
FARRAHER**
AND **TAMMY DREW
HOIDAL**

Copyright © 2011 Laura Drew Farraher and Tammy Drew Hoidal
All rights reserved.

ISBN: 1463736789
ISBN-13: 9781463736781
Library of Congress Control Number: 2011912870

CreateSpace, North Charleston, SC

Youth comes but once in a lifetime.
—Henry Wadsworth Longfellow

CHAPTER 1

Twenty dollars. That's how much parents have to pay every five minutes they are late to pick up their kids at Beverly Hills Private School. Many parents don't mind breezing in and writing the eighty-dollar check for being twenty minutes late. But it's fun to watch some of them squeal up to the front of the school, jump out of their cars, and sprint inside, checkbooks in hand.

The teachers with late duty are the crankiest in the school. I'm sure Mr. Consuelos, our school principal, knowingly assigns Mrs. Winch and Mrs. Stickney this nightly position to deter parents from abusing the system. "Students are to be picked up promptly by 6:00 p.m." reads the first page of the BHPS Student-Parent

Handbook. But, as we all know, even parents just can't seem to abide by the rules sometimes—my mother included.

It's always the same three at school well after dark. There's Anthony Bryant, son of Maxwell Bryant, the award-winning rapper and actor. Anthony's our class clown and will do anything for a laugh. He gets in trouble all the time, but the teachers have his dad on speed dial and can call him any time for backup support. His father is really strict, so if he gets a call, Anthony gets in big trouble.

Then there's Natalia Steins. She's gorgeous. Her father is African American and her mother is Swedish, so she has caramel-colored long hair and beautiful golden skin with bright blue eyes. But the nice thing about Natalia is that she doesn't realize how pretty she is. She's actually really shy, and it's rare to catch her smiling. Her father is a well-known music producer, and her mom is a famous model.

And then there's me, Clementine Constantine Borealis Calloway. I'm tiny for my age, thirteen. I'm way too skinny. I guess I dress OK, although my best friend Esther says I haven't found the style that expresses my inner spirit yet. My hair is to my chin; my mom says I'm too young for extensions, but my hair is too thin to grow long. It's dark blond, but I wish it was light blond like my mom's. Mom says that when I turn fifteen, we can talk about chemical changes to my hair.

I'm an OK student. I hate math, but I love, love, love English class because we do a lot of writing. And I really love writing. I don't have a father. Well, I have one, but my mother says she has no idea where he is. She met him hiking in Arizona when she was in her early twenties. Whenever I ask about him, she says, "Clem, all that really matters is that you were conceived out of love." Gross.

Oh, and did I mention that my mother is a world-famous rock star?

CHAPTER 2

Mom was born with the name Deborah Grace Calloway. She grew up in a part of Brooklyn, New York called Bushwick. Her mom up and left when my mom was fourteen. From what I understand, my grandmother wasn't a very nice woman. I guess she drank a lot and could be really mean to my mom and grandfather. My mother doesn't talk about her too much, but she once told me that it was not uncommon for her to come home from school and find her mom passed out on the couch. If Mom accidentally woke her up, my grandmother would scream at her and tell her what a failure she was. "Why can't you be more popular and get decent grades like Nancy from down the street?" she would yell.

"I'll try, Mom," my mom would reply as she tried to cover her with a blanket. "Get some sleep and we can talk about it later."

"Don't tell me to get some sleep," my grandmother would say. "You just want me to sleep so you can lie around and watch television."

"No, Mom, I'm going upstairs to do homework. Oh, and I got a B on my math quiz today, and Mr. James didn't even warn us ahead of time that we were having it. That's a pretty good grade for a pop quiz."

But by that time, my grandmother would be asleep and drooling down one side of her face.

My mom's father was a construction worker, and, as she recalls, "that man worked so hard his hands would bleed." She used to soak them in warm water when he got home and then put cream on them for him. They were very close, and he felt awful that my mom didn't have a real mother to raise her.

"You know," he'd say, "your mom's just sick. That's all. One of these days, she's gonna get herself out of this slump and get herself back to the way she used to be, when I met her. Boy, she was pretty. You should have seen her, Debbie. She could stop traffic. And was she nice. She used to volunteer all the time at the church, you know."

"Yes, Dad. I know." Mom had heard the stories countless times, but she could never remember her mother being pretty or nice. She always remembered her as she was now: a drunk.

It was on a Sunday that my grandfather and mother returned from church and found my grandmother gone. She had packed up her things and left, without even leaving a note. My mom has never tried to look for her; she says that she just assumes her mother probably drank herself to death somewhere. I guess my grandfather never stopped believing that one day she would return and be the woman she used to be. But that never happened.

I don't remember my grandfather. I wish that I did. My mom says he was the kindest man on earth. He used to say to everyone, even strangers, "Have you heard my Debbie sing? She has the voice of an angel." And she does. From a very early age, Mom sang at church. On Sundays, she would lead the children's choir and always sing solos. Everyone would lean toward one another and whisper, "Boy, that girl can sing." And my grandfather would say, "That's my girl."

When my mother turned sixteen, she used to pretend that she was eighteen and sing at bars on the weekends to make extra money. She didn't tell her father because he would never have let her. She told him that she babysat. He appreciated the money she gave him and would say, "You work too hard for someone your age. Always have."

It was at one of those bars, the Big Easy, that a tall, handsome, bronze-skinned man with dark hair walked in one night. It was T. J. McGilvary, one of the most famous music producers in the world, and he just happened to be in Brooklyn celebrating the birthday of one of his old friends.

It's a good thing my mom didn't know who he was or she probably would have been really nervous when she sat down with her guitar that night. But she wasn't nervous. She just sang her heart out and nearly knocked Mr. T. J. McGilvary off his chair, so the story goes.

He found her when she was finished packing up her things. "How old are you?" the man in the black suit asked. T. J. McGilvary always wore a black suit, even to casual events like ball games.

"Eighteen," she said.

"No you're not." He knew she was lying. "I'm going to ask you again. How old are you?"

"Seventeen," Mom replied.

"Do you know who I am?"

"No, I don't. Should I?" she asked, becoming a bit annoyed because it was getting late.

"Yes. I'm the man who's going to make you a star. What's your name?"

"Debbie. Deborah, actually. Deborah Calloway."

"Well, we'll need to do something about that," McGilvary told her. "You need a name fit for a star."

And he did make my mom a star, after he christened her Gray Calloway. By the time Mom turned eighteen, T. J. McGilvary had produced her first number one hit, "I'll Always Be Yours." And the next year, her album went platinum. She moved to Los Angeles, much to the dismay of her father. But he knew with her success, Los Angeles was the place to be. She won two big awards—one for Best Song of the Year, the other for Best New Artist.

But success came with a price. A girl that young, living in Los Angeles by herself, just screamed trouble. She began drinking and going out to clubs, and the media watched her every move. They called her "Gray, Miss Partaaay," and it seemed like every time she was on TV, it was because she was doing something she shouldn't.

My mom blames that time period on "too much pressure for a young girl from Brooklyn." It seemed like everyone was just waiting for her to spiral out of control—and she did. I don't know the whole story because it was before I was born, but I'm pretty sure she may have used drugs too. She stopped performing and recording, and one day her manager, Mondella, found her at her apartment. The door was wide open, and my mom was on the bathroom floor, barely breathing.

Mom was taken to the hospital, and they called my grandfather, who flew to Los Angeles immediately. He wanted to bring her back home to Brooklyn, but Mondella told him that the media would follow them and my mom would not get the rest and peace that she needed. So the alternative was to have her go to a retreat in Arizona. Mondella told my grandfather that the place was amazing. It had horseback riding and hiking, yoga classes, and, most importantly, privacy. Plus, there were people there who could help her get better so she could eventually return to Los Angeles and do what made her really happy—sing. So that's where she met my father, in Arizona.

Over the years, the tabloids have speculated who my father might be. And each year it seems like they tag someone new. I know he was at the Arizona retreat "finding himself," just like my mother. I know he was about the same age as my mom. And I also know that he was not famous. My mom has always said that he was a big reason she got well. But whenever I ask Mom if we can find him, she always says, "Clementine, he didn't ask to be a father. He didn't want a life in the spotlight. When you're grown up, perhaps we can talk about it, but right now it's just not fair to do that to the man."

Two months later my mom was back in Los Angeles, and from everything I've heard, she came back with a bang. She recorded again and released two number one singles. My grandfather had moved from Brooklyn into her Los Angeles apartment to make sure she stayed grounded. And he was also with her when she went to the doctor because she couldn't shake the stomach flu. She found out that day that she was three months pregnant. "Well," my grandfather told her, "this is a sign from above that you're not the most important thing in your life anymore. It's a sign that you need to put this baby first, and that means taking care of yourself."

Whenever I ask Mom if she was happy when she found out she was pregnant, she always says, "I was definitely shocked, but the minute I found out, I just knew that I was going to have a daughter, and she was going to be my best friend."

Mom says that my grandfather was amazing when I was born. He would get up in the middle of the night to give me bottles. He'd sit with me for hours and rock me to sleep. I wish I could remember him. He died when I was two of a massive heart attack. He just fell asleep and never woke up. But Mom says he died a very happy man because she had gotten herself better, but mostly because he was so happy being a grandfather. I bet he would have been like a father to me. I sometimes like to talk to him, to tell him how I've been or what my mother's been doing to annoy me recently. And, somehow, I think that he hears me. I really do.

CHAPTER 3

Tonight Mrs. Winch seems especially annoyed as she stares at us and then at the clock, then rolls her eyes, sighs, and looks back at the clock. "These parents," I hear her mutter, "they think that just because they are so-and-so, the rules don't apply to them."

Mrs. Stickney nods in agreement with a look of disgust, then shakes her head at the three of us.

It's Thursday and I am beyond excited. Tomorrow night is the Spring Fling dance and I am going with the hottest guy in the seventh grade. His name is Gabriel Farthing, and he is cute, smart, funny, athletic, etcetera.

It is very rare that Mom picks me up from school, but months ago she promised that we could have a special girls' night because of the big dance. Shopping, manicures, pedicures. "You name it, Clem," she'd said. "We're gonna make you so fabulous that Garret won't know what hit him."

"Gabriel," I'd reminded her. How could she not remember the name of the love of my life?

It is 6:23 when the door of the lobby flies open. In runs Anthony's mom. Even in a black Juicy sweat suit with her hood up, she's gorgeous. She's on her cell phone and mouths to Mrs. Winch, "How much do I owe you?" Mrs. Winch writes a big "$85" on a sticky note and holds it up. Anthony's mom digs through her studded alligator purse, pulls out a wad of bills, and hands them over. She motions to Anthony—without even a hello—to get his things and hurry. Out the door they fly.

"You ready for the dance, Clem?" asks Natalia in a voice so soft I can barely hear her.

"No, not yet. But Mom's taking me shopping tonight. I can't wait. I'm thinking spaghetti straps, but simple. *Teen Vogue* says dark colors are in this season. Are you ready?"

"Oh, I can't go. We're leaving tomorrow for Paris. My grandmother is back in the hospital, so we have to go visit her."

"Oh, that's awful. Is she sick?"

"Kind of. She's got mental issues. When we see her, we have to look at her through a window. And the entire room is like a pillow so she can't hurt herself. She won't know who I am. My mom will cry. My grandmother will scream swears at us in French. And then we will leave."

"Wow. That's awful."

I try to think of something to say that will cheer her up, but then a man in a black suit and black hat swings open the door and peeks his head in. "Come on, Talia. Let's go." It's her driver, Bentley. He tells Mrs. Stickney to bill the Steins family and disappears out the door.

"Bye, Clem," she says in her sweet voice. "Have fun at the dance."

"Thanks, Natalia," I answer. "See you when you get back."

I watch her head toward Bentley and give him a half-smile. She's wearing a plaid Burberry coat and matching beret. Her long honey-colored hair is curly and almost messy-looking, but any girl in our class would kill to have it. Again I think how pretty she is—and how much prettier she is when she smiles.

CHAPTER 4

Oh, dear God. I know that noise anywhere. It sounds like a metal rod being dragged down a chalkboard, followed by loud bangs. It is Marina's car.

Please no. Please no. Please no.

Maybe Marina forgot that Mom is picking me up. Or maybe it's not her car. Or maybe Mom borrowed Marina's car. That's crazy. My mom has seven cars. Why would she borrow Marina's car?

I don't dare look out the window. I just wait. The door swings open and there he is. Jesus-Marco, Marina's four-year old son. He is wearing jeans and a Hulk tank top frayed at the shoulders to show his scrawny biceps, and he's eating a green lollipop that he has managed to break apart, putting a portion in his nose. And he's laughing hysterically. Marina comes rushing in behind him. She is short, probably my height, but plump, with wild black hair that she tries to control in a bun.

"So sorry, Clementine. My car won't go fast today. I push on gas. It does nothing but make big banging noises. I have to have Carlos," her husband, "fix it once and for all."

"Marina, did you forget?" I say. "Mom's picking me up tonight. You don't need to be here."

"Si, senorita, but Mommy called me. She had to leave town urgently. She said she will explain later. But she send money to get you pretty for the dance. I take care of you."

She reaches out her hands and summons me toward her. Jesus-Marco snorts out of his nose and the green blob of lollipop lands on Mrs. Winch's desk.

"So sorry, senora," Marina says. "Could you please bill Ms. Calloway?"

Mrs. Winch and Mrs. Stickney look at her disapprovingly and send us out the door, locking it behind us.

CHAPTER 5

Strapped in Marina's backseat, I feel carsick before we've even left the parking lot. Her car smells like diapers and french fries. The windows are tinted too dark and it's difficult to see outside, which usually helps when I'm queasy. Jesus-Marco is attempting to smear the remainder of the gooey green lollipop on my arm while eating a chicken nugget that he's found buried in his car seat.

"Where are we going?" I yell over the salsa music blaring from Marina's radio as we turn right on Robertson Boulevard.

"Oh, I know just the store. My cousin get married and she find the most beautiful dress at this store on Alejandro."

I've never heard of that street. We pull up to a pink building that has several scary-looking mannequins in the window. The sign reads "Foxy's." The clothes look like they're straight out of a 1985 sitcom.

"Are you sure we shouldn't just go to the Beverly Center?" I ask.

"Trust me, senorita, you love it. We make you gorgeous."

I squeeze out of the backseat and follow Marina through the door. We're greeted by a large woman with big red hair and tons of lipstick.

"Hola, Marina! Como estas? Look at Jesus-Marco. The little man so big! And this must be Clementine."

"Hi," I say quietly and try to hide behind Marina.

"Clementine," Marina says, "this is my good friend, Rosario. She will find perfect dress for you."

"Oh, just call me Ms. Foxy," says Rosario. "Come with me! Come with me! I have beautiful dresses for you. Do you like purple? You would look gorgeous in purple."

She pulls me into a dressing room. Hanging on the door are four dresses, all bright colors—aqua, green, purple, and hot pink.

"Hot pink is very popular this season," Ms. Foxy says.

Hmm, I hadn't heard that.

"You try these on and come out when you have them on. We will be waiting!" She steps out of the dressing room.

I take the green dress off the hanger first and hold it up to myself. The tag reads size eight.

"Excuse me, Ms. Foxy?" I say. "These dresses are size eight. I wear junior sizes or size double-zero in women's."

"Oh, no problem," she says. "I cut dress to fit you. I am like fairy godmother before your ball. Trust me. Trust me. Just try them on." She closes the dressing room door.

I hesitantly undress and step into the green silk dress. It's covered in sequins and has frilly, puffy sleeves that are bigger than my head. I zip it up the back as best I can. I can barely walk because it's so long, and the top part hangs well below my training bra.

"Come out, come out!" Ms. Foxy says. "We want to see!"

I can't believe this is happening. I picture Esther right now at the Beverly Center—probably in Neiman Marcus—trying on fifty adorable Betsey Johnson dresses.

I slowly open the dressing room door and step out.

"Ahhhh! You are beautiful!" screams Ms. Foxy.

"Oh, I'm going to cry," Marina gasps, her hands covering her mouth. "My little Clementine looks all grown up."

"You look like a big, stinky frog!" yells Jesus-Marco.

I frown. "You know, I just don't think green is my color."

"OK, OK, you go try on purple, you will love it." Ms. Foxy nudges me back into the dressing room. I'm very relieved to take off the green dress.

The purple dress is strapless. I've never worn a strapless dress because, as Mom tells me, "you need something to hold it up, honey, and you may have to wait a few years for that." But she did say that last year; perhaps I've magically transformed into a woman who could wear a strapless dress.

I unzip the purple dress, put each foot into it, and carefully pull it up under my armpits. Weird—this dress doesn't have a tag and it looks like there's someone's make-up on the inside.

I try to zip it in the back. I can't reach, so I stick my head out the door and motion to Marina for help. She pulls me out and screams, "Ahhhh! This is the dress!"

"Please just zip it, Marina," I ask when I see Jesus-Marco staring and giggling from the corner of the store.

She zips it up; the two women stand back and gasp simultaneously.

"La niña preciosa!" whispers Ms. Foxy.

"Um, but what about the top?" I ask. I pull the bodice out in front of me to show that I clearly don't have the chest to fill this dress out.

"Oh, don't worry, senorita, we have cutlets," Ms. Foxy says.

"What?"

"Cutlets. Everyone wears them. All celebrities. Britney. Beyoncé. Everybody wear cutlets." Ms. Foxy disappears into the back of the store and returns with two rubbery beige things that look like raw chicken.

"You see? Cutlets. Feel. So real. No one will ever know."

I reach out and take one. It feels like squishy rubber and is shaped like a half-moon.

"What do I do with them?" I ask.

Before I know it, a cutlet is strategically placed on each side of my training bra. Marina and Ms. Foxy once again stand back and gasp.

"Look in the mirror!" Ms. Foxy turns me around, and there I am, in a strapless dress. And it totally fits.

Why hasn't anyone ever told me about cutlets before? This is life-changing.

CHAPTER 6

I go with the purple dress and cutlets. Surprisingly, it pretty much fits everywhere else. Ms. Foxy stitches it at the bottom so I won't step on it when I walk, but other than that, I'm surprised at how much I like it. I think it's probably because I've never looked so big in the bust before. Ms. Foxy even gets out the make-up stain with soap and water. As we're leaving the store, I hear her ask Marina if I need a spray.

"What is she talking about?" I whisper.

Ms. Foxy hears me and answers, "You know—spray. So you not so pasty white. Every celebrity sprays. Jennifer. Beyoncé. Even I bet your mommy sprays."

"Oh, you mean a spray tan," I say. "Yes, my mom has Victoria from the spa come to our house. But it's quite a long process."

"Oh, no, no," Ms. Foxy says. "My spray booth only take five minutes." She turns and motions me to follow her.

She leads me to a back room filled with brown boxes, a small kitchen with a microwave and mini-refrigerator, and, in the corner, a big white booth labeled with air-brushed letters, "Spray it, sexy!"

"It's easy," Ms. Foxy tells me. "You get in booth naked, and it tells you what to do. You get undressed. Get in, tell me when you're ready, and I push button."

"Wow, that sounds easy," I say. "I wonder why my mom doesn't have one of these at home."

Marina, Jesus-Marco, and Ms. Foxy leave the room so I can undress. I step cautiously into the booth. It's cold. I don't know where I should put my hands. Above my head? Down by my sides?

"You ready, senorita?" Ms. Foxy asks.

"I think so," I say.

All of a sudden, a gigantic blast of brown vapor explodes from the wall of the booth. It's OK, I think. It will probably rotate and circle around my whole body.

Then I hear a loud robotic voice say, "Girar a la derecha."

What? What does that mean? Maybe it means stand still. I was moving around a little. Before I know it, another blast covers the left side of my body again. Then the voice says, "Salga la cabina."

And then it's silent.

"All done!" yells Ms. Foxy.

"I don't know if I did it right!" I yell frantically.

"It's fine. That machine work so well. So much gas. It gets all of you, don't worry. Dry yourself off with towel and we wait for you at front of store."

So maybe the vapor filled the booth and soaked into my skin. I do feel damp all over. I dry off, step out of the booth, and put my clothes back on.

I suddenly feel butterflies in my stomach. A strapless dress, cutlets, and a tan—Gabriel is going to be so into me.

CHAPTER 7

When Mom is in town, it seems like our house is always filled with people. It's kind of like when a person gets home from work and they have dogs that have been waiting for them all day. The person comes home, and the dogs are jumping all around, yipping away, wagging their tails, and following the person from room to room. That's like my mom—but instead of dogs, she has people. They all remind me of yipping Chihuahuas circling her, asking what she needs, or telling her how great she looks.

But when Mom's out of town, the house is really quiet. Almost too quiet for me. That's why I like that Marina spends the night when Mom's not here. And even though Jesus-Marco makes me crazy, it doesn't bother me when he sleeps over. We have this one guest bedroom that's painted like a jungle. Mom calls it her safari-theme bedroom. Jesus-Marco loves to sleep in there. It has life-size animals painted on the walls: elephants, zebras, monkeys. And the king canopy bed has mesh all around it and really soft blankets.

When Mom is out of town, Marina lets me sleep with her in her room. Even though she doesn't live with us all the time, she has her own bedroom and kitchen. It's cozy in there, and, to be honest, our house is so big, it creeps me out to sleep all alone in my bedroom when it's so quiet and empty.

It's pretty late when we get home, and even though my mother forbids TV-watching unless approved by her, Marina lets me sneak it when I sleep in her room. Our favorite is *Nancy Grace*. Marina always says, "That Nancy Grace, she don't take no nonsense from no one. You want to know who should be president? Nancy Grace."

Tonight I nod my head, half-asleep. My head is resting on my left arm, and I realize that it smells weird.

"Marina, what is that smell?" I ask. "Smell my arm. Does it smell like bologna?"

"Oh, it's just spray tan, Clem. It go away after you shower. Don't worry."

That's true. I'm sure the smell will go away, but Ms. Foxy instructed me not to bathe for twelve hours. I drift off to sleep thinking about the Spring Fling and me dancing in my strapless dress with Gabriel.

CHAPTER 8

It's 9:00 a.m. when I hear Marina calling me from the kitchen. "Come, on sleepyhead! Breakfast ready! I make your favorite—waffles with strawberries!"

Yum. That does sound delicious, and I'm positive that I got a good night's sleep so I will look extra rested for the dance. Marina put my slippers next to her bed and I slide my feet into them. I wonder what dress Esther picked out. I'll have to call her and find out. We usually talk or text about fifty times a day, which completely annoys my mother. But she is worse than I am. She has three cell phones, Skype, and assistants that make phone calls for her. She says, "Clem, if I could get rid of all my phones, I would. But it's my business. Someone has to pay the bills."

When I make my way to the kitchen, Jesus-Marco is sitting at the granite island eating a huge bowl of Froot Loops. He stops munching when I walk in, immediately points at me, screams, and laughs uncontrollably.

"Oh, grow up, Jesus." I know I have bed hair, but so does everyone at nine in the morning. But he doesn't stop. In fact, he yells, "Mommy, Mommy, Clementine half brown! She like Dora on one side!"

My heart beats faster. What is he talking about? I look at Marina in desperation and I see her hands cover her mouth.

"Oh, my mother of God," she whispers.

I sprint to the bathroom off the kitchen and flick on the light. I look in the mirror. Oh, my mother of God is right! I am half dark brown, and the other half of me is my normal color, pasty white with a few scattered freckles.

I freak. "Ahhhhhhhhhhh! Marina! Help me!"

She runs in behind me.

"It's not so bad, senorita," she says. "We fix it. We fix it."

At this point, I'm sobbing uncontrollably. Jesus-Marco is doubled over laughing, pointing and yelling, "Half-Dora! Half-Dora!"

"You stop that, Jesus!" yells Marina. He puts his hands over his smile in an attempt to cover his sheer joy.

Within minutes, Marina is on the phone with Ms. Foxy. I hear her talking nervously as she paces the floor, saying things like "She has important dance tonight!" and "Her mommy going to kill me!" She notices I am listening and begins speaking in Spanish, giving me a fake smile and thumbs-up sign.

I'm sitting on the bathroom floor with my knees up to my face when she reenters with instructions written on a sticky note.

"OK, senorita," she says, "we need to go to the market to get some things to put in the bathtub. It will take brown right off."

This makes me feel a little better, but the thought of going anywhere looking like this makes me absolutely nauseous. But I know Marina is not allowed to leave me at home alone. Strict orders from my mom, who, by the way, I have not heard from in two days.

Marina hurries us into her car. We're still in our pajamas, and Jesus-Marco is now just staring at me, smirking. "You smell like burnt nuts," he says.

"Oh, shut up," I snap back. "You always smell."

When Marina starts the car, it once again sounds as if it's going to explode at any moment. As we start down the driveway, the muffler drags, sparking as the gates open and we drive out onto the road.

Thank goodness Walgreens is only minutes away. When we pull into the parking lot, I immediately state to Marina that I am not, and I mean *not*, going into the store.

"OK, OK," she says. "But don't tell Mommy I leave you in here. Jesus-Marco stay too. I be five minutes. Keep the doors locked."

She races out of the car. I notice that she, too, is in her bathrobe, which almost brings a smile to my face. But then I remember I am half brown and want to cry again.

Jesus-Marco finagles his way out of his car seat and climbs into the front seat.

"What are you doing?" I yell. "Get back here! I'm telling your mommy!"

He doesn't seem to hear me as he pushes every button and turns every knob he can get his hands on. The Latin music is now blaring, so I reach forward to turn it down. Jesus-Marco then goes to push the door lock. Suddenly, the loudest siren-sounding alarm I've ever heard goes off. It is ear-shattering, and I have no idea how to turn it off. It sounds like someone has attached an ambulance siren to this car, which is probably exactly what Marina's husband has done. Why would this car need an alarm? Who is going to steal this heap?

Jesus-Marco covers his ears as I push every button I can find to turn off the alarm.

I look into the store window to see if Marina hears us, but I don't find her. What I do see is a giant black Suburban pulling up into the space next to us.

Please don't let it be anyone I know. Oh, God, please.

But as my lack of luck would have it, I see Blaire Michaels and Paige Carlton hopping out of the back-seat. They are ninth graders. Super-popular ninth graders. I hear Blaire say, "What's wrong with that car?"

I am on my knees, crouched down in the backseat.

Please don't look in here. Please don't look in here.

And then I hear Mrs. Michaels' voice through Marina's car window.

"Is everything all right in there?" she asks as she squints into the windows. "Are you kids OK?"

CHAPTER 9

Maybe if I just crouch on the floor of the car, Mrs. Michaels will go away. I hold my breath; I'm not sure why. She can still see me. And she can clearly see Jesus-Marco because he has his face pressed to the glass, blowing on it and licking it.

"Girls," I hear Mrs. Michaels yell, "don't go in yet, I need to make sure these kids are OK. Someone has left them unattended, or they may have been abducted. Either way, this is against the law."

Oh, my God. Oh, my God.

I peek up for just a moment to see Mrs. Michaels, Blaire, and Paige staring through the glass at me.

Blaire leans in for a closer look. "Clementine? Is that you?" she yells.

Oh, God. Oh, God.

I slowly slide up onto the seat. It's difficult to hear anything over the blaring siren alarm, but I wave and nod.

All of a sudden, Marina appears.

"Oh, so sorry! So sorry! That stupid alarm. Carlos need to fix that! It's crazy! Jesus-Marco, why are you out of your seat? You get your bum back there!"

Marina has plastic bags in her hands and almost doesn't notice Mrs. Michaels and the two girls looking in at me.

"Excuse me, are you Clementine's caretaker?" asks Mrs. Michaels.

"Si, si," Marina nods. "We need some lotions to take brown off her skin. Too much spray tan."

I see Blaire and Paige giggling; Mrs. Michaels gives them a swift glare.

"Well, I'm sure that Ms. Calloway would be very upset if she knew that Clementine was left unattended in a parking lot in Los Angeles," Mrs. Michaels scolds.

Marina looks as though she will cry. "Oh, I was just three minutes, senora."

"Do you know what can happen in three minutes? Abduction. That's what can happen. I will call her. Where is she? Let me guess, not in town."

Mrs. Michaels rants on and on about half the mothers in LA who shouldn't have kids unless they can take care of them.

I want to protest and tell her that my mom is a good mom, but the words won't come out. I'm so angry. Angry that I am half brown. Angry at Mom for being away and not taking me shopping. Angry at Mrs. Michaels and Blaire and Paige for pulling up next to us. Angry at Marina for getting me into this mess. Oh, and angry at Jesus-Marco—well, just for being Jesus-Marco.

CHAPTER 10

While soaking in a tub of rose oil, salt, sugar, vinegar, and several other ingredients, I make two phone calls. The first is to Esther. She can always make me laugh when I need it most. And, boy, do I need it now.

"You're soaking in what?" Esther asks.

"Some sort of potion to take my spray tan off."

"Did you have it done at the Spa Tropicale on Rodeo? I heard that they're amazing. I'm surprised they messed it up like that."

"No, I didn't have it done at a spa. I had it done at a store called Foxy's."

"OK, well that was a huge mistake."

"Esther, I called you to cheer me up, not bring me down. Do you understand that this is the most important day of my life and it is ruined?"

"Don't worry, don't worry. It will come off. And if it doesn't, we can totally bronze the other side. My mom has this great Bobbi Brown spray bronzer."

"Ugh. The thought of spraying anything at all on my body totally creeps me out."

"I bet it's not that bad. I'll be over at five. We'll get ready together. You'll look fab. Trust me."

"Thanks, Esther. And I still have the cutlets and cute dress."

"You are so lucky. My mom won't let me wear cutlets until I'm sixteen. She says only hoochies wear cutlets."

"Thanks, Esther. See you at five."

The next phone call is to my mother. Her assistant, Hali, picks up. "Hi, Clem."

"Hi," I say in my most depressed-sounding voice.

"What's up?" she asks, sounding busy. I hear lots of voices in the background.

"Is my mom there?"

"She is, but she's onstage rehearsing. She feels really bad about missing out on your prom weekend, but the Rolling Stones' agent called and asked her to surprise Mick by singing 'Happy Birthday' at their show. It's going to be so hot."

"They still sing? What is he, like, ninety?"

"Clem, they're legends. Have a little respect."

"Please tell my mother to call me. Tell her it's very urgent."

"It always is, isn't it? Will do, Clem. Have fun at the prom."

"It's a dance, Hali."

"Oh. Dance."

With that, I hang up and attempt to lower myself further into the tub. I put half my face under the water, as well, because that, too, is still dark brown.

CHAPTER 11

The doorbell rings and I hear Jesus-Marco scream, "I get it! I get it!"

Jesus-Marco is completely in love with Esther because she is nice to him and pats him on the head and says, "Oh, you're so cute!" If she only had to spend more than one day with him.

I hear her climb the stairs to my bedroom, and I take one last look in the mirror. Marina has managed to blend half of my face and upper body using her base foundation called Tahitian Heat. I now totally look like full-blown Dora, but at least both sides of me match. And the dim lighting at the dance should also work in my favor.

"Holy hotness!" Esther stands in the doorway, her eyes wide with excitement. She's holding a pink plastic bag. "You don't look that freakish at all, and that dress is the bomb!"

Esther looks amazing in a short black wool dress and shiny black Escada kitten heels. Suddenly, I feel deflated. Maybe I shouldn't go to the dance. Sensing my somber mood, Ester playfully hides the bag behind her back.

"I've got a surprise that will totally cheer you up!" She hands me the bag; it reads "Hair on Melrose."

Ooh-la-la! That salon is *the* best place to get your hair done. I reach in and pull out a clump of long black hair. The tag reads "Real Human Hair," which grosses me out a little.

"Wow," I say. "Thank you, Esther."

Esther smiles excitedly. "It's an extension! For the dance!"

"Um, Esther, my hair is dark blond. This is jet black, like your hair."

"Don't you know anything? Lowlights are totally in right now. It's going to look amazing. And it will attract attention to your hair and not your skin."

"Good point."

Esther sits me down in front of my vanity and goes to work. I watch her in the mirror and admire her long, silky black hair. It hangs down to the middle of her back, and there is never a hair out of place. She's donated her hair to Locks of Love several times, and it always seems to magically grow back within a month. One time, while getting my Parisian bob—the look that Victoria tells me works with my face—I asked if I could donate my hair to Locks of Love. Victoria sighed and said, "We better keep what we have, hon. It's just not enough."

I feel sharp stabs to the back of my head as Esther rams the comb up and down to attach the hairpiece. "Ta-dah!" She hands me a mirror so I can see the back.

"Not bad," I say with surprise. "Not bad at all."

My hair has never looked so long or thick. Granted, the color is definitely off, but it feels so good swishing on my back.

"So Edward is picking us up in an hour," Esther says. "I told him we definitely need to be twenty to thirty minutes late to make an entrance. You told Gabriel to meet you there, right?"

"Yes, I just couldn't deal with the thought of picking him up with Jesus-Marco in the car. Not to mention that if I pulled up in Marina's death box, his parents would freak and not let him go."

Esther's brother, Edward, is the coolest. He is a junior in high school, and—despite being smart, captain of the baseball team, and popular—is totally nice to us. She's so lucky to have a big brother. Or just a family that's always around, for that matter.

CHAPTER 12

Edward drops us off at the entrance of the Wilshire Hotel at 7:20. Butterflies whirl around in my stomach; I still can't believe that Gabriel is actually my date! He asked his friend Preston to ask Esther to ask me. I totally thought she was joking, but turns out it was the real deal. My skin has been looking fantastically clear over the past few months with the help of a kit that Marina ordered me from an infomercial that a hundred teen stars had endorsed. And recently, Mom gave me the green light to wear lip gloss and a touch of eyeliner. A little make-up does wonders.

We hurry out of the car and Edward peels out of the parking lot before we can even thank him for driving us.

"Hi, girls!"

Miss Betsy, my math teacher, is at the door, obviously assigned greeting duty this evening. Miss Betsy is like many of my teachers, very pretty and hopeful that one day she will catch a big break in the acting industry. At our school, with the exception of Miss Lyle, who teaches English, teachers come and go. Sometimes your favorite teacher will one day midyear just not report to work. Then Mr. Consuelos will sit at the teacher's desk and grimly report that so-and-so has decided not to teach anymore, which usually means that he or she landed a sitcom or something. I learned early on not to get too attached to any one teacher. Except for Miss Lyle. She is different. She went to college to be a teacher and doesn't want to be anything else. I make her reassure me of this on a weekly basis.

We stop in the lobby to chat with some friends—and then I see him. Gabriel is over in the corner with none other than Blaire and Paige. I'm sure they're telling him all about the incident at Walgreens.

"Well, go over there!" Esther nudges me toward him.

"In a minute. I don't want to look like Miss Desperate! Let him find me," I insist.

"True, true. Let's do a lap."

As Esther and I make our way through the crowd, I feel a tap on my shoulder.

"Hey." It's Gabriel!

"Hey," I reply, trying not to seem too eager.

"A bunch of us are headed upstairs to grab Mountain Dews. Do you want to come?"

"Yes! I mean, sure, OK." I give Esther my OMG! look when Gabriel turns around, and she tells me she'll catch up with me later.

I follow Gabriel—along with Paige, Blaire, and three of his guy friends—to the steps.

"Did your nanny get her alarm situation straightened out today? I think my ears are still ringing," asks Paige while we're walking.

I roll my eyes. "Oh, yeah, that car. I mean, seriously."

"I can't believe your mom let's you ride around in that circus show with those people," adds Blaire.

Those people? What does she mean by that?

I feel my face get red, which is clearly not a good thing given my foundation and spray tan. I have to stop myself from yelling something really nasty back at her.

"Permission slips? No access to the upstairs restaurant without permission slips."

It's Mr. Parker. He's the man assigned all of the crap work at school. Playground duty, lunch duty, early morning—like 6:00 a.m.—duty, photocopying, etcetera. He also makes extra money by opening up a snack shop at lunchtime. He sells cups of noodles and adds hot water for us for three dollars. Given the long line that always forms at his shop, I'm thinking Mr. Parker makes out pretty well.

Everyone pulls out folded-up papers and hands them to Mr. Parker. "Thank you, thank you," he nods and lets each student go by.

"You did remember a permission slip, didn't you?" asks Gabriel.

"Um, totally," I stall. "I'll go get it. It's in my coat. You go ahead and I'll meet you upstairs."

Gabriel disappears up the steps.

Crap! I knew I forgot something!

Everyone knows that the cool kids usually spend most of the dance upstairs at the restaurant, not on the actual dance floor. And you need a permission slip to get into the restaurant.

I find Esther already out on the dance floor and tell her that she needs to go with me to the bathroom—*immediately.*

I tell her my dilemma as we reapply lip gloss. She turns me toward her and says, "Whatever you do, don't forge a note. Last year, Lindsay Cohen got suspended for it. They totally know somehow; it's like they learn how to spot forged notes at teaching school or something."

She's right. My best bet is to just hang out down-stairs. Plus, it'll make it look like I'm blowing Gabriel off a little, which Esther says is a good thing.

Esther and I dance for a little while, but she tells me to cool it because I'm sweating a little and my make-up's beading up on my forehead. After fifteen more minutes in the bathroom to fix my make-up, I emerge to find Gabriel standing in front of me.

"Where were you?" he asks.

"Oh me? I decided I wasn't thirsty, so I just hung out down here."

"Oh, OK." He looks a little puzzled. "Do you want to dance?"

"Yes! I mean, sure, yeah, whatever." I try to calm down and remind myself not to go too crazy on the dance floor or I'll sweat my make-up off again.

Thank goodness. A slow song. Gabriel puts his hands around my waist and I put mine around his shoulders. I catch a glimpse of Esther dancing with Leon Willibury, a very nice kid, but not someone Esther would ever go for. His hairline comes up to her chin, and he wears headgear, this circular device that attaches to his teeth and wraps around the back of his head. I didn't even think dentists tortured kids with headgear anymore; apparently his dentist hadn't gotten the memo. But

Esther being Esther, she was kind enough not to say no when he asked her to dance. She smiles and gives me the thumbs-up. I smile back.

I can smell Gabriel's cologne and think he must have put it on especially for me. I wonder if he smells the Coco perfume that I had squirted on my neck. Mom always says it's a classic that men can't resist.

Suddenly, I hear the deejay yell, "Let's get this party started!"

He blasts a Britney song and everyone jumps up and down and waves their arms in the air.

I do the same and try to keep a smile on my face, but my dress is not feeling right. The portion that Ms. Foxy pinned feels loose, and cool air is coming into the dress. I lower my arms and try to just sway to the music, but Gabriel takes my arm and spins me around.

"This song rocks!" he yells.

Back and forth he yanks me to the beat of the music. Then suddenly I know something is terribly wrong. My left cutlet has dropped out of the side of my dress. It's now on the floor next to my foot.

Oh, dear God. Oh, dear God. What do I do?

I'm in a complete state of panic and think I might hyperventilate. I pull Gabriel's arm and yell, "Let's go dance by Esther."

"Right on," he agrees and follows. We leave my cutlet in the middle of the dance floor.

Somehow my dress manages to stay up despite the missing cutlet, and I leave Gabriel dancing with Esther and a group of friends while I dash to the lobby. I find the black cardigan I'd brought.

Thank God.

I'd almost left it at home. I put it on, button it up, and check out my reflection in the darkened window. Not bad. I run to the bathroom to fix my make-up and catch my breath. After a few minutes, I head back to the dance room. Esther meets me at the entrance.

"Clementine, we need to talk," she says with a look of horror on her face. "Are you missing something?"

"Yes!" I whisper. She can tell I'm about to cry.

"OK, OK. Don't worry. This is not a big deal, but I will tell you that the eighth grade boys are playing pass with a cutlet on the dance floor as we speak."

"Oh, my God! Oh my God! What do I do? Let's go. Let's just go home. I'll text my mom's driver right now."

"Don't be crazy. You'll look insane. And no one knows it's *your* cutlet. The cardigan is genius! You can't even tell. The boys don't even know what the thing is. Just act like nothing is wrong. Trust me."

We head back to the dance floor, Gabriel, and the game that's ensuing. Anthony Bryant has the cutlet and is waving it around his head to the beat of the music. He yells, "Catch!" and tosses the cutlet. To my horror, Gabriel jumps up and grabs it.

"What is this thing?" he laughs and throws it like a football to his friend across the room.

"Weird, I don't know," I say with a fake laugh.

After fifteen minutes, Mr. Parker makes his way onto the dance floor and says, "Alright, alright, give me that. We're not here to play ball. Someone's going to get hurt."

Andrew Libby hands over the cutlet, and Mr. Parker almost drops it. He seems a little freaked out. "What is this?" he sputters. "Whose is this?" Then he turns and carries it off the dance floor, holding it like you would a dead mouse, way out in front of him. I'm not sure what becomes of it after that.

I've had enough. I'm really hoping that I can just say goodnight to Gabriel and leave him thinking about how great I am. After all, he hasn't really noticed that I'm brown on one side and now half-flat. I seem to have escaped the cutlet ordeal. But when Gabriel walks me outside, things get even worse.

"Well," he says, "thanks for going with me to the dance. It was pretty fun, for a school dance."

"Yeah, it was," I nod.

I can't stop wondering if he's going to kiss me. My first real kiss—it would be perfect. And if he kisses me, it would mean I'm totally his girlfriend.

"Well, goodnight," he says, leaning in toward me.

Oh, my God! He's going to kiss me!

I close my eyes and open my mouth just slightly, like I've seen it done a million times in movies.

Suddenly, my hair is pulling toward him.

"What the hell?" he asks, jumping back.

Gabriel yanks his arm away from me, but my head follows his arm up and down as he tries to free himself. I feel excruciating pain, but I barely notice because I'm so mortified. My hair extension is hooked to his wrist.

"What is this thing?" he asks, trying to yank the long black hairpiece off his watch. It's completely tangled.

"Can you just stop shaking your arm for one second?" I plead. My head is bent over, and the more he shakes his arm, the more tangled the hair seems to get.

"What's going on over here?"

Oh, my God. It's Mr. Parker. Doesn't he have anything better to do? Like go home?

"Um, I think I'm stuck," I say, my face now red because I'm almost upside down.

"Can't you just take that thing off your head?" asks Gabriel.

"Yes, if you give me a minute and stop moving, I'll try."

People gather around, and most of them are laughing and pointing. Mr. Parker is trying to help, but he's making the situation worse by the minute. He's created a huge knot around the hair extension. Finally, Esther finds us and tells Mr. Parker to let her handle it. She works for at least five minutes before my head is free and I can stand up.

The giant clump of tangled black hair is still attached to Gabriel's watch.

CHAPTER 13

"**O**K, you need to call him," says Esther after we finish our breakfast Sunday morning. "And soon, because my mom's going to be here to pick me up."

"What do I say? I feel like a total freak."

"First of all, no one knew that was your cutlet. Secondly, the hair extension thing? That could happen to anyone. Even Paris Hilton has been known to get hers stuck in doorways."

"Really?"

"Really. Now, when you call him, you need to be funny. Edward told me that older guys love girls who are funny. That's why Gabriel is always hanging out with Blaire and Paige. They say funny things all the time."

"Seriously? I think they're witches."

"Well, Gabriel doesn't. So trust me. We need to think up something funny for you to say, especially if you get his voice mail, which hopefully you will. Then it puts the ball in his court."

We get out a notepad and start brainstorming.

"OK, what if you tell him that on the way home we stopped by a rad party that was broken up by the police?" suggests Esther.

"No, not believable."

"OK, what if we tell him we got a flat tire, Edward snapped, his girlfriend Mitzi jumped out of the car, and we had to huff it home in kitten heels?"

"Brilliant!" Esther is so smart.

I rehearse a few times then dial Gabriel's number. It immediately goes to voice mail, and I give Esther a happy thumbs-up.

"Hey, It's Gabriel. You know the drill." *Beeeep.*

"Hey, Gabriel. It's me, Clementine. Clementine Calloway. Um, just wanted to call and let you know that last night was a great time."

I look at Esther nervously, and she mouths, "Funny!"

I look down at the notepad and start to read.

"Well, you should have been there on the way home. Esther's brother picked us up and—"

Beeeep.

"Oh, my God, Esther! It cut me off! I didn't even tell the whole story!"

"You have to call back. You can't just tell him part of the story. That was so not funny!"

"I know! I didn't know it would cut me off mid-sentence!"

"Here, I'll dial, just continue where you left off. It's not a big deal." She hands me the phone.

"Hey, it's Gabriel. You know the drill." *Beeeep.*

"Hey, Gabriel. It's me again, Clementine. I think I got cut off. Anyway, I just wanted to tell you that you totally should have been in the car with us last night. Esther's brother picked us up and when we got into the car—"

Beeeep.

"Nooooo! It did it again!" I almost burst into tears.

"Why are you taking so long to get to the funny part? That's why it's cutting you off. Just get to the part when my brother's girlfriend jumps out of the car! That's the funny part!"

"I can't call back now. There's no way."

"If you don't call back, it's going to be totally weird. The story is not even funny. He won't even laugh. At least if you call back and finish the story, it will be funny and make him laugh." She hands me the phone.

"Are you sure?"

I can't believe this is happening. Isn't the spray tan, cutlet incident, and hair extension mishap enough for one weekend? Why do I have the worst luck of any girl in Beverly Hills?

"Yes, I'm positive. Now call."

I close my eyes and hit redial.

"Hey, it's Gabriel. You know the drill." *Beeeep.*

"Hey Gabriel, it's Clementine again. I can't believe I just totally keep getting cut off—" Esther motions for me to speed it up.

I look down at the paper frantically and begin speed-reading.

"So I was in Esther's brother, Edward's, car and we were in the backseat and Esther's brother's girlfriend, Mitzi, was in the front seat. Anyway, all of a sudden the tire blew! Well, Mitzi freaked and—"

Beeeep.

"It cut me off again!" I cry in panic.

"OK, but at least you kind of got to the funny part," Esther assures me.

"He is going to think I'm such a freak."

I drop to the floor and throw the phone across the room.

"I think he'll call you back," she says, patting my back.

"There is no way he is calling me back."

CHAPTER 14

Gabriel does call me back, about two hours later. It's completely awkward, and he tries to tell me that the hair thing wasn't that big of a deal.

"But actually, I'm really just calling about tickets," he finally says.

"Tickets?" I ask excitedly. Maybe he's going to take me to a show or concert. "What do you mean?"

"Well, I heard that your mom is going to cap off her tour at the Staples Center. And Blaire and Lauren told me that if I took you to the dance, you could probably get us all tickets."

It's all beginning to make sense now. Why would Gabriel ask me to the dance anyway? He could go with anyone. He asked me because of my mom.

"You mean you took me to the dance so you could get concert tickets?" I hoped he couldn't tell that my voice was shaking.

"Well, kind of. I just thought I would do you a favor, and then you would do one for me in return."

In all of the movies I had seen, and books that I read about love, not once did the guy ever say, "Hey, I'll hang out with you if you can score me concert tickets."

"Yeah, sure, I'll see what I can do."

My heart sinks, and I'm not sure if I even say good-bye as I hang up the phone.

CHAPTER 15

Mom returns home Sunday night. I'm on the couch trying to concentrate on homework when she sneaks up behind me.

"Hi, baby! Mommy's home!"

She's wearing a long, gray cashmere cardigan, tight jeans, and black boots that come up to her knees. Despite having just gotten off an airplane, she looks beautiful. Her hair's in a tight bun, and she's wearing her tortoise-shell glasses. I love when she wears her glasses because it makes her look more like a regular mom than a rock star.

For a moment, my anger at her for deserting me on such an important weekend seems to disappear.

Something about your mom being home just feels good. But I know I have to tell her how my life is utterly ruined because of her trip to sing with the Rolling Stones.

"I want to hear all about it," she says. "How was the dance with Greg?"

"Gabriel, Mom, it's Gabriel. And it was awful. It was the worst weekend of my life."

"Oh, wow. How about a cup of acai-pomegranate tea to cleanse the toxins from your soul? It always works for me."

"That's disgusting. Never. And Mom, why are you talking with a British accent again? You know that drives me crazy."

"Well, you spend time in London and that beautiful language just rubs off on you."

"Mom, you spent a week there last summer. I'm with Marina all the time and I don't speak Spanish."

"For what I pay her, you should speak Spanish—and Chinese and Russian, for that matter. But back to this weekend. What happened?"

I tell her everything, from the pickup on Friday to Foxy's spray booth, the trip to the pharmacy, the permission slip I didn't have, the cutlet and hairpiece, and, lastly, the phone call.

And to my surprise, she sits and listens to the whole story. She even shuts off her phone when it rings.

By the time I'm finished, I'm sitting with my head on Mom's shoulder and full-blown sobbing. After I've finished and blown my nose, she tries her best to console me.

"Clementine, my spiritual guru, Autumn Flower, tells me that our soul is like the sky. Sometimes, dark clouds like to creep in and cover the sunlight and positive energy. But the sun is too strong, and eventually those clouds either rain or dissipate. Do you understand what I'm saying?"

"No." Why can't she just talk like a normal human being?

"Clem, it may seem like the end of the world, but I promise you, it will pass. Gabriel is a bonehead for not appreciating you. And he wants tickets to my show? Then he can pay three hundred bucks like everyone else. And I'll make sure they put him in the nosebleed seats."

This brings a smile to my face, and I put my head down on her lap. She strokes my hair and then says, "Clem? No more cutlets or spray tans for a while, OK?"

"OK."

I can never stay mad at Mom. Sometimes I wish she was a normal stay-at-home mom like Gabriel's, but I know that will never happen. I learned early on to snuggle her close while she's in town because the very next day she'll probably be someplace very far away.

CHAPTER 16

It's Monday morning, and, to add to my misery, Jesus-Marco is beginning school at Beverly Hills Private today. My mom's decided that she will fund his education, a scholarship of sorts, given the fact that he's like family to us. I remind her that there are some fantastic private schools just down the street from mine.

"What about the Lycée Français?" I say. "Jesus-Marco could learn French!"

"Clementine Constantine Borealis Calloway!"

Here we go, the full name. I'm going to have to sit through one of Mom's speeches.

"Jesus-Marco and Marina are family. Marina's been with us since you were a baby. Her son deserves to have a great education, like the one you are getting. I don't know what I'd do without Marina, and it's the least I can do. Now I want you to watch out for him. School can be a mean place for new kids who start midyear."

"Fine. But it's not like he's my brother."

"Clem, be nice. That's all I'm asking."

"Well, he better not embarrass me when he sees me."

"Oh, he won't. Marina says he is a wonderful and very well-behaved student."

I almost spit out my orange juice. I could never picture Jesus-Marco being wonderful and very well-behaved.

Mom drives me to school, which I'm really excited about, even though she is a notoriously bad driver. Once at our beach house in the Hamptons in New York, she forgot something, ran inside the house, and when she got back outside, the car was in our pool. True story. There were helicopters circling over the house for days and reports in the paper that she had killed herself by driving into the pool. She just laughed and said, "If I were going to take myself out, driving into a swimming pool is not the way I would do it."

I like being in the car when it's just the two of us because it makes me feel like she's an ordinary mom, like all the other moms driving their kids to school. We blend right in. No one stops, whispers, or stares. No one surrounds us or asks for autographs or takes pictures.

We are just a normal mom and daughter when we're in the car.

But sometimes we have to be careful. Many times, the paparazzi, the crazy photographers, will follow us and we'll end up back at home. Mom gets so flustered because they drive up right beside us, so close that they almost hit us. She'll yell, "Clem, hold on!" then step on the gas and head straight home. But this morning, we take one of the new vehicles, a white Escalade with dark windows.

"I don't think they'll know this car," Mom says, "at least for a few days."

The paparazzi are actually a lot better with Mom than they are with some of the younger stars. She says it's because she's boring and doesn't do anything to make them all want to sleep outside her house. She usually has two or three photographers following her around, and they're usually always the same guys. She knows them by name and isn't afraid to get in their faces and say things like "You know what, Dan? Tomorrow morning, I'll be at your house when you and your family wake up, and I'll follow you guys around all day with a camera in your faces." They'll respond with comments like "Hey, Gray, I'm just doing my job. I didn't sign up to be a rock star like you did."

My mom likes to have a little fun with the photographers and magazines. Sometimes she'll carry books when she knows that she's going to be followed. For example, last month she was photographed with a book titled *When You Are in Love with an Older Man* and the tabloids went nuts. Who is the older man? Is it someone famous? Little did they know, she just did it to drive them crazy.

"Are you sure Henry shouldn't just drive us?" I ask. Henry is Mom's driver. He's been with us as long as I can remember.

"We'll be fine, and besides, I gave Henry the day off. Let's go or you're going to be late."

I'm surprised that it's just the two of us getting into the car, that doesn't happen very often. "What about Rocco?"

Rocco's my mom's bodyguard. Well, actually he's our bodyguard. Sometimes people are crazy and come up to us on the streets, like they think they know us or something. And it can be scary, especially if one person turns into dozens of people screaming and calling your name. Rocco's job is to keep everyone at a distance. And he's very good at it. He's not much of a talker, but he has always been very nice to me. He's gentle, gigantic, and bald. He always wears black from head to toe and a big diamond earring in one ear, a Christmas present from my mom a couple of years ago. When people see him with us, they definitely think twice about coming too close. He reminds me of a lion defending his cubs, and I'm often glad that he's around.

"Clem, I'm driving you to school, not taking you across the country," Mom says. "We'll be fine."

When the gates open and we pull out onto the street, we don't see anyone following us, which is a good sign. There are four touristy-looking people standing across from our driveway taking pictures, but I don't even think Mom notices them.

"Starbucks?" she asks.

"Definitely," I reply, thinking a hot cider with whipped cream is just what I need to get my day going. Not that my mom would let me order anything else, except for maybe hot chocolate.

Mom leans out of the car. She's wearing her incognito outfit—dark sunglasses and a Lakers baseball cap.

"I'll have a grande green tea with raw sugar, room temperature, with a slice of lemon on the side, and could you put that in a venti cup? And my daughter will have a tall hot cider with whipped cream."

There's a long pause, and I'm imagining the Starbucks baristas rolling their eyes and mimicking Mom's crazy-long order. We zip around the corner and drive up to the window. A college-age boy is standing there in his black apron and visor. He has bad skin and wears very thick glasses. He gives us a super-big "Good morning! How's your day going?"

"Great, thanks," Mom answers quietly, not making much eye contact. She's pretending to rummage through her purse. I watch his face, and, as usual, it's like a lightbulb comes on over his head. His eyes widen, his mouth opens.

"Are you who I think you are?" he asks, his voice quivering.

"Well," Mom says, trying her best to be friendly, "that depends on who you think I am." I've heard this song and dance about a million times.

"Are you Gray Calloway?" he asks, looking around, trying to beckon his coworkers to the window.

"Yup," she says quietly, "and I don't mean to be rude, but I've got to get my daughter to school. Is our order ready?"

"Yes, yes, Ms. Calloway. He disappears and suddenly there are four Starbucks workers at the window, smiling and waving. Then we see a woman, probably the manager, shoo them all back to work. She passes our drinks out the window.

"Sorry about that, Ms. Calloway. You've just got some big fans in here."

"Not a problem," Mom says. "How much do we owe you?"

"On the house. Thanks for stopping by our Starbucks."

Mom puts a twenty in the tip cup, waves, and pulls away.

"You know, it kind of bugs me when they do that," she says. "I spend more money tipping in that jar than if they'd just let me pay for my drinks."

We listen to classical music in the car. Whenever we listen to the radio stations I like, usually one of Mom's songs will come on. And she doesn't like hearing her own music, believe it or not. She says she's too critical of herself, and it makes her want to plug her ears. I tell her that if I had two songs in Ryan Seacrest's top ten this week, I'd blast them with the car windows down. She just laughs and rolls her eyes.

"What's up for this week?" I ask as we pull onto Beverly Boulevard.

"Rehearsals all week. And I'm still auditioning dancers for the tour. Some of the dancers these days, they march right in like they own the place. They just can't believe it when we tell them they didn't make the cut. They literally throw temper tantrums. Can you believe that?"

My mom recently released a greatest hits CD, so she's going on a five-city tour, which isn't bad. Usually she'll have to hit something like sixteen cities. This time, she'll be going to London, Tokyo, Sydney, New

York, and ending it in Los Angeles. Tickets went on sale last month and sold out in every city within four minutes. I know I won't see her for a whole month, and when I do, she will be exhausted, too thin, and weepy because she "misses me so much."

And I'll be stuck in Marina's backseat with Jesus-Marco. I already feel carsick. And I'm wishing Mom didn't have to leave me again.

CHAPTER 17

Somehow, Miss Lyle can tell that something is wrong. She stops me as I'm walking into her third period class.

"What's up, Clem? You OK?"

"I'm fine."

"Well, good news. We got a delivery over the weekend. And, even better, I've got an important announcement to make today that might interest you."

Yay! I bet it's our pen pal letters! A letter from my cross-country BFF is just what I need to lift my spirits.

Miss Lyle grew up on an island off the coast of Maine. Maine's up really high on the right-hand side of the United States. The only thing I knew about Maine before Miss Lyle and my pen pal was that it's freezing and people eat lobster there all the time—like, even on Thanksgiving.

I remember the first day Miss Lyle showed us pictures of Chebeague Island, the place where she grew up. I thought it looked absolutely beautiful.

"Were you, like, Amish, Miss Lyle?" asked Anthony Bryant when she was telling us that her island had no traffic lights, hospitals, or malls.

"No malls?" Esther gasped. "How did you survive?"

Miss Lyle laughed and replied, "We found plenty of other things to do besides shopping. That's for sure."

"But what if you got sick and needed emergency medical care?" asked Leon.

"Well, there are two ferries. The ferries run about every two hours to and from the mainland. Once you get on the mainland, the nearest city is only about ten minutes away. And there, Leon, you will find a hospital. And a shopping mall, Miss Esther."

Anthony was still dumbfounded. "What about In-N-Out Burger?"

Miss Lyle shook her head.

"Starbucks?" asked Anthony, without raising his hand.

"Nope," she replied as several students gasped. "But Mrs. Higgins, my neighbor, was known to make *the* best coffee and hot chocolate on the island. And she would leave her door open for us to drop in and fill up our cups."

"Are you for real? She just left her door wide open so any psycho could just march in and swig down her hot chocolate?" Anthony asked, completely shocked.

"Anthony, hand in the air for comments. But yes, on the island, everyone knows everyone. And everyone looks out for everyone else. No one would think of stealing from or hurting a neighbor."

"Miss Lyle?"

"Yes, Anthony?"

"Did you grow up on *The Little House on the Prairie?*" Everyone laughed and Anthony clearly beamed with pride.

"No, Anthony. But it was a really nice place to grow up."

Since that first day, we have had multiple talks about Chebeague Island. I've learned that it's only about five miles long and three miles wide. There is an elementary school on the island, and usually kids only have about six students in their classes. Kindergarten through third grade's in one room, and grades four, five, and six are in the other.

I've learned that it's not always freezing in Maine, that there are four real seasons. Snowy, cold winters with blizzards. A rainy spring that brings tiny flowerbuds all over the island. A warm, humid summer, just right for swimming at one of Chebeague Island's many beaches. And fall, which to me sounded the most magical of all, when the leaves change to brilliant shades of red, gold, orange, and yellow. Miss Lyle's parents, who still live on the island, sent us a box of leaves in October, and we put them up on our bulletin board. I had only seen leaves that color in magazines. I would often walk by the bulletin board just so I could reach out and touch them. Eventually they dried and cracked, but, to me, they were still beautiful.

But one of the coolest things about Chebeague Island is the fact that my BFFPP, Best Friend Forever Pen Pal, lives there. Her name is Morgan Rich and she is fabulous. We are so much alike, it's almost like we're sisters separated at birth. She loves to write, just like me, and she also told me that she has her own style, which I think is super cool. And she also only has one parent, just like me. Her mom passed away two years ago from breast cancer. I think that's so sad. But her dad sounds really nice, and he also travels a lot for work, like my mom, so we also have that in common.

The only weird thing is that Morgan doesn't text because she doesn't have a cell phone, and she's not allowed to e-mail yet. She wrote that she doesn't have a computer at her house anyway. I would go insane without my phone and computer; I don't know how she does it. Though I haven't seen a picture of her, she says that she has brown hair and brown eyes. She also wears glasses. I bet they're like the cute Chanel specs that came out this season.

The closest I've ever been to Maine is Boston, and I don't remember it because I was three. My mom had a concert there. I once asked Mom if she would schedule a concert in Maine, to which Hali replied, "Are you kidding? The trip there would not bring in enough money to make it worth it. There aren't enough people in that state. And why would you want to go to Maine anyway, Clem? I've heard it's absolutely freezing there."

"Hmm," I retorted. "I don't remember asking you, Hali. I thought I was having a conversation with my mother."

"Don't be fresh, Clem," my mom replied. "Maybe one day we'll take a trip there. I've always wanted to go to Maine. Where is Maine?"

CHAPTER 18

Miss Lyle has long blond hair that she usually wears in a ponytail or sometimes a messy bun with a pencil stuck in it. When you see her, you know instantly that she's not from LA. She usually wears khakis with an argyle sweater and always loafers or clogs. Sometimes she'll wear plaid skirts with an oxford shirt. Esther says that Miss Lyle does the preppy thing perfectly. She looks like she could be in movies because she's that pretty. She reminds me of a short Gwyneth Paltrow.

Miss Lyle's first name is Colby. She says that she was named after the small, beautiful college in Maine where her dad went. "Maybe someday you'll go there, Clem," she once said to me with a smile. Miss Lyle is the best thing that ever happened to Beverly Hills Private School. Even though she is strict, she works hard to make sure that we learn all we can in her classroom. Not only that, she's introduced me to poetry. And not just any poetry, poetry that means something.

I love that poetry can be unpredictable. "Just like life," Miss Lyle says. You think you're reading about a dude on a sled in the night trying to get somewhere in a hurry when all of a sudden he stops dead in his tracks just to enjoy the scenery.

I remember the day when Miss Lyle read us the poem about the two plums in the icebox by William Carlos Williams. Even though it was so short and simple, I felt like I could just taste the sweet, cold plums. And then we read poetry by Maya Angelou, who I think is amazing, and if I could meet her, I would probably cry.

"Poetry is for girls," said Anthony one day while Miss Lyle was passing out a new poem. "I don't know why we need to read it."

"Oh really?" she said, her eyebrows raised.

"Really," he replied adamantly and pushed the handout to the corner of his desk.

"And what do you think of rap?" she asked.

"I love rap. Rap is the bomb."

"And you don't think that rap is poetry?" she asked.

"No, it's not girly. It's hardcore music."

"Hmm. Well, does rap usually rhyme?"

"Sometimes, I guess," he replied.

"Is there usually a message, something the singer is trying to tell you?" she pushed further.

"I guess."

"Well, if you printed out the lyrics to a rap song, I think you'd see that it is very much like a poem."

"Well, it ain't no plum in an icebox poem, that's for sure."

The class giggled.

"It *isn't*—remember, we don't say ain't in this classroom. Anthony, your assignment tonight is to ask your dad what he thinks of poetry and tell us about it tomorrow."

"I think he'll say poetry is for wusses," Anthony replied.

"Well, we'll see. And I want the truth. You know I'll call him if I need to."

"Yes, Miss Lyle."

I wonder what my mom thinks of poetry. I've never asked. She writes music, too. I never thought of music as being poetry before. But I guess it is; it's just poetry matched with the right sounds.

The next day in English class, Miss Lyle asked if Anthony had anything to report to the class. When he nodded, without making eye contact, she motioned for him to stand up and read the crumpled piece of paper he was carrying.

"OK, Anthony, let's hear it," said Miss Lyle, folding her arms in front of her.

He began to read. "If it were not for Gwendolyn Brooks, a famous African American poet, my dad would not have become a rapper. When my dad was thirteen, his teacher read a poem in class called 'We Real Cool.' It was then that my dad realized that if you gave words rhythm and made them mean something, the possibilities were endless. He said that Miss Brooks wrote about issues that mattered and the feelings that came from her heart, which weren't always happy feelings. So that is why Gwendolyn Brooks will always be special to my dad."

He folded up the paper and sat down.

Miss Lyle smiled, and then she clapped her hands.

CHAPTER 19

Miss Lyle moved to California after she graduated from the University of Maine. She came to Los Angeles to be with her college boyfriend, who had been drafted by the Los Angeles Kings, a professional hockey team. Shortly after, he was traded to the New Jersey Devils. Miss Lyle was already teaching here and told him that she couldn't just pick up and leave. Rumor has it they broke up because he thought she should move with him, that his job was more important. But Miss Lyle believed that her job was just as, if not more, important than skating around with a puck. That makes me like Miss Lyle even more because I think most girls would have definitely followed their hockey-star boyfriend to wherever he was playing. After all, he's probably making big bucks. She could have just sat on the bleachers and cheered him on with all the other hockey girlfriends and wives, wearing super-fashionable clothes and jewelry. But she wanted to teach, and she wanted to keep her commitment to our school, to her students.

And for that, I am so grateful.

CHAPTER 20

So Miss Lyle's big announcement is probably the most exciting news I've ever heard.

"OK, class," she begins, "I have something important to discuss with you, so I need your full attention. That means you, Anthony."

He's busy searching through his backpack for who knows what.

"Why you always busting on me?" he shoots back.

"Hmm. I hear your dad's in town this week. It would be really easy for me to get ahold of him. I'm sure he'd love to see what you've been up to today in class."

That's all it takes. Anthony sits up straight and gives a quiet, "Yes, Miss Lyle."

But back to the big announcement.

"Seventh graders at Beverly Hills Private School have an amazing opportunity. My best friend, Sarah White, teaches at the school we've been pen palling with on Chebeague Island. We had a long phone conversation last week and came up with a fantastic idea. I've OKed it with Mr. Consueleos, and he says we should give it a go. We are looking for any students who would like to take a ten-day trip to Chebeague Island, Maine, this June. You will stay with a host family, which may or may not be your pen pal's. I will be going to chaperone and plan daily activities while you are there."

I almost jump out of my seat. I raise my hand.

"I'll go! I'll go!" I scream.

"Clem, not so fast. You need permission from your parents first, so I have some forms for you all to bring home."

I can see it now. Morgan and me sitting on the beach, reading the latest teen magazines, doing each other's nails, hitting the local island hot spots for dinner. It would be fantastic. I would definitely need an entirely new wardrobe for this island getaway. Perhaps some easy, breezy tropical dresses and hip foul-weather gear!

CHAPTER 21

"You are out of your mind if you think you are going to go flying off to some island across the country with some teacher I barely know and stay with some family I've never met!"

Mom has her arms crossed, and I know it's going to take everything I have to convince her to let me go.

"Mom, this is an educational trip. We will be learning about island living and marine biology. Not to mention you will be on tour, so I would just be sitting at home by myself anyway."

"You are never by yourself, Clementine. Marina will be here. And Jesus-Marco. And how do I know this man you're staying with isn't some sicko? This is just insane, Clementine."

"Mom, this is an opportunity for me to grow and connect with people of a different culture. Morgan's dad is a single parent, just like you. And Miss Lyle said that her house is just down the street. If I feel uncomfortable, I can always go stay with her. She said so. Wouldn't you rather have me on the beaches of Maine learning about crustacean life than at the Beverly Center shopping for the eight hundredth time?"

"Clem, you are not just an ordinary girl. You need to face the facts that I am who I am, and there are crazy people out there who could hurt you. Do you know how many people write letters to me on a daily basis, threatening me? I don't tell you because you don't need to worry about that. But I do."

"Mom, my pen pal has never even heard of you. Miss Lyle says that everyone knows everyone on the island, and they'll know if anyone suspicious is around."

"Well, I'm going to have to have a long talk with Miss Lyle. I am not even remotely saying yes right now, Clementine, so don't get your hopes up. Marina! Get me the school phone number please!"

Yes, yes, yes!

I know I'm getting closer and closer to going. If anyone can convince my mom to let me go, it's Miss Lyle.

She'll reassure Mom that I'll be safe. I cross my fingers as Marina hands Mom the phone and the number to our school.

After a very lengthy conversation—and my mom asking Miss Lyle one hundred questions, like "What is the crime rate on the island?" and "Are you sure I shouldn't send Clementine with a bodyguard?" and "Perhaps the students from the remote island in Maine would enjoy an all-expense-paid trip to LA instead?"—Mom hangs up the phone, crosses her arms again, and looks me straight in the eye.

"I'm really nervous about this, Clementine," she says. "You're all I have." Her eyes are tearing up, so I walk over and hold one of her hands.

"Does this mean I can go?"

"I can't believe I'm saying this, but, yes, this means you can go."

CHAPTER 22

Given that it's the end of May and I'll be leaving for Maine on June 14th, I only have to survive a little more than two weeks in Los Angeles before my Maine adventure could begin. I've already begun packing and have decided to take extra clothes, in case Morgan wants to do any swapping while I'm there. Returning to Beverly Hills with a new Maine style would make me totally hip in the fall.

Jesus-Marco's attending Beverly Hills Private has actually been a good thing, because he's diverted attention away from me and onto him. He's already on a weekly check-in, which means Marina has to sign a report from his teacher every Friday. I wonder if the school realizes that she really can't read English very well and that most of the time she just signs it or asks me to read it. Sometimes I make up stories, like Jesus-Marco stripped down to his underwear and ran through all the classrooms. Marina almost drives off the road, swearing in Spanish, before I tell her that I'm just joking.

"Oh, Clementine, you going to give me heart attack!" she says.

But Jesus-Marco does get in a lot of trouble. One time he found a pole that went with some of the gym equipment on the playground. He started spinning around with it over his head, yelling, "I am a chopper from Iraq!" He hit two kids in the head before coming to a stop. Luckily, no one was seriously injured, but Mr. Consuelos had Jesus-Marco sit in his office for the entire day.

Another time, Jesus-Marco loaded up some potato chip snack-packs from my house and brought them to school. He proceeded to sell them on the playground for two bucks each before Mr. Parker caught him and brought him to the office. I guess Mr. Parker doesn't want any competition.

As for Gabriel, with the exception of the occasional "Can you pass me the glue?" in art class, I pretty much do not exist. But my hair extension fiasco has been the joke of the school since the dance. Paige Carlton likes to walk by me in the hallway and yank her hair in the air and yell, "Clementine, got any new hair extensions?" Esther just glares at her for me while I ignore her.

At home it's just me, Marina, and Jesus-Marco at night now, since Mom's in full-blown rehearsal mode. Papers report that this is going to be her biggest and best tour yet, possibly her last.

"Is that true, Mom?" I asked during one of her rare moments at home. "Is this your last tour?"

"I don't know," she said. "Some days I feel like I'm getting too old for this. Those sixteen-year old singers have a lot more energy than I do."

But somehow I know that she won't stop any time soon. My mom can't sit still long enough to watch a movie, so even if she stopped singing, I know she'd find something else to do that would take her away from home. And take her away from me.

CHAPTER 23

There is one cool thing about the end of the year at my school—the Summer Kickoff Carnival.

Last year, the carnival was so much fun. Mr. Consuelos went all out and rented a jumping house, cotton candy machines, and even a dunking booth for Mr. Parker. Parents were encouraged to volunteer, so it wasn't uncommon to see famous basketball players manning the jumping house or soap opera stars handing out cotton candy.

When I finally get a chance—between rehearsals, of course— to ask Mom what she's going to do to volunteer this year, she gives me that "don't bother me now, Clem" look.

"I heard that Anthony Bryant's dad is going to dee-jay," I say morning while eating breakfast at our kitchen island. He's one of the world's most famous rappers; if anyone's busy, it's him.

"Clem, he's not touring in June," she says as she's applying lipstick in front of our kitchen mirror.

"But he is making a movie."

"In Los Angeles. Look, I will do my best. You know I will. Hey, I know—how about we get that Garrett in the dunking booth? I've got a great right arm, you know."

"Gabriel. His name is Gabriel. And I'm done with him. I told you that."

"Oh yeah, I forgot. Well, it would still be fun to dunk him." And with that, she's out the door.

"True," I say out loud and realize I am talking to myself because she is already gone.

CHAPTER 24

I decide to wear my skinny jeans with the little pink
T-shirt I'd just picked up at the Third Street Prom-
enade to the carnival. Esther assures me that Gabriel is
a big loser for asking me for concert tickets, especially
since he still has my black hair extension.

"That thing was not cheap," she says, shaking her
head as we get ready in the school bathroom.

"I don't even want to think about it, Esther," I say,
applying some Cherry Jubilee lip plumper.

"Is your mom coming today?" Esther asks.

Her parents are helping out with the food table, and
by helping out, I mean donating most of the food. Her
parents' restaurant is known as one of the best Korean

barbecues in the country. It's an LA hotspot for celebrities and famous athletes. But I like it because when Esther and I go there to eat, her mom always treats me like one of the family. We'll sit at a huge table in the back where beautiful Korean ladies cook steak, shrimp, and whatever we want right on our table. Mrs. Cho, Esther's mom, always rubs my back and asks me if I need anything, and I smile and shake my head no. It's enough to sit there with Esther's family, watch them laugh and sometimes argue, and just feel what it would be like to be part of a real family. Esther's dad is quiet; her mom's clearly the boss in the restaurant. When she speaks, all the staff jumps. Esther's parents are strict, but it's obvious they love their children fiercely.

Then Esther's mom, still rubbing my back, would ask me, "Your mommy fly away again?"

"Yes," I would reply, looking away.

"Aw, she love you very much. She must miss you so much. She amazing woman. I send you home with some seaweed soup for her. She needs to take care of herself."

"Yes," I would reply, "thank you."

Why are people always trying to reassure me that my mother loves me?

"Clem, Clem, you ready?" Esther's waiting for me at the bathroom door. "Let's go. I guess Anthony's dad had to jump on a plane to New York, so he hired DJEZ

Epsilon to deejay. He's supposed to be the bomb. Do I look OK?"

Esther's wearing an adorable plaid miniskirt with a little white cardigan that ties in a bow in the front. Mr. Consuelos has agreed to let students change out of our uniforms and have free dress for the carnival after school.

We walk out to the play yard and smile—it's completely transformed. There are two jumping houses and even a mini-roller coaster. Mr. Consuelos can really throw some fabulous events. I see him at the back of the playground, running around sweating and pointing to Jaime and Paul, the two custodians, where he wants the huge flower arrangements to go.

"What do you want to do first?" Esther asks.

"How about we just do a lap and check things out?"

"Perfect," she agrees.

The playground is crowded, given that all of the students are here, even the babies. Two-year olds are the youngest class, and they look like babies to me. I can't believe that some of them are dropped off at seven in the morning and then picked up at night when it's already dark. I kind of wonder why their parents even had them if they can't spend any time with them. But then I remember that people probably ask the same thing about Mom and me.

Suddenly, music blares from the speakers, and all the kids jump up and down and cheer. I can see DJEZ Epsilon in his white sweat suit with dark sunglasses and tons of gold necklaces. He looks like a celeb, even though I've never heard of him.

"All right, Beverly Hills Private School, you ready to paaaaaarty?" he yells into the microphone.

Again, we all cheer and clap.

"OK, then get your asses on that dance floor!"

Esther looks at me in shock. "Did he just say asses?"

I laugh and can't believe my ears. "I think so."

EZ starts dancing and suddenly we hear the song "Shake Your Fine Ass" by Chronic Funk, as loud as it can get. All of the kids, even the little ones, are dancing. But the parents and teachers all have wide eyes and are whispering things to each other, like "This is not appropriate" and "Do you think we should say something?"

EZ climbs to the top of a massive speaker with his microphone and Big Gulp and screams, "Shake your young teacher thangs in the air and wave your hands like you just don't care!"

Within seconds, I see Miss Lyle whisper something to Mr. Consuelos, who's oblivious to the music. He's busy trying to show a parent how to use the popcorn popper. I watch his face turn beet red as he storms over to the speaker.

As Mr. Consuelos reaches the deejay booth, EZ puts his hand up and yells, "Whoa, whoa, whoa, back off, little man! It's time to blow the roof off this mother!"

Mr. Consuelos yells and flails his arms, although we can't hear what he's saying.

Within minutes, EZ jumps down off the speaker and announces, "Looks like we gotta turn things down a notch. Didn't know I was deejaying at a convent!"

Esther and I look at each other and giggle. This is hysterical.

Other than that, the carnival goes really well and everyone seems to have a blast. I keep looking at the entrance to see if Mom will show, but I already know somehow that she won't. When she says she'll try her best to make it, it usually means not a chance. Esther and I ride on the roller coaster about ten times, and then we were going to jump in the jumping house, but Blaire made some comment we overheard about only babies jumping in a jumping house. So we decide to play some games instead.

After the carnival, most of the kids go home with their parents. The rest of us pack up our stuff and sit in the office. Jesus-Marco sits in the seat next to me. His face is covered in cotton candy. He looks over and sticks out his tongue. I look away.

And even though it bums me out that Mom didn't show and I have to go home with Jesus-Marco, I'm not that upset. I know that in just a couple of weeks, I'll be on that plane to Maine. And I know it's going to be the best trip of my life.

CHAPTER 25

In my online Maine research, I learned that the days would probably be pretty hot, but the nights would be brisk and cool. Perfect. I could sport my cute sundresses and new tankini by day, and then switch to warm and cozy evening attire at night. I'd have to pack plenty of shawls, wraps, and my new Gore-Tex breathable North Face shell.

Morgan told me in a letter that one of her favorite things to do at night is to go see live music. How cool is that? Live music on an island? I can just picture it. The two of us swaying in a crowd of Maine concertgoers, maybe even catching the eye of a hot local boy. He will come and offer his coat and say that I look cold—and beautiful. A summer Maine romance. I would be the talk of Beverly Hills upon my return.

Morgan says that their house is small but has a lot of "rustic charm." I'm not sure what that means exactly, but I know Mom likes to call our Hamptons house rustic, with its five bedrooms and a guest wing. I wonder if Morgan has a pool or if we will just be beaching it everyday. Either way is fine for me. I'm just excited to meet my new Maine BFF in person. I know that we will be as close as sisters after my trip there. We will stay up all night talking about writing, our friends, and, of course, boys.

Esther calls me this morning and asks that she not be replaced as my BFF. I tell her that I only have one California BFF and that will always be Esther.

Only three more days—I can't wait!

CHAPTER 26

So the two other students going on the trip are Leon Willibury, the short kid with the headgear, and Ebony Cooper, a really nice girl who sits behind me in English class. Both her parents are plastic surgeons, they have a show on TV called *Surgeons to the Stars.*

When I ask Ebony if she's excited about the trip, she gives me a nervous smile and says, "Kind of."

"It's going to be great," I assure her. "We can totally sit together on the plane and watch DVDs."

Esther wanted to go, but her grandparents will be visiting from Korea. Secretly, I think it's probably a good thing that she isn't going. I know that I probably wouldn't be able to bond with Morgan as much if Esther were there. Esther might be a little jealous of the two of us, and that would be hard to deal with.

Mom has arranged her schedule so she can go with me to the airport. I know it's nice that she did that, but I just know how airport trips with my mom can be. The paparazzi love airports. I don't know why they think the shots of celebrities at LAX are so fun to look at. They always snap photos of tired, make-upless stars who just want to go home and not be bothered.

"Are you sure?" I ask Mom. "Because Miss Lyle said that she would drive me."

"Are you kidding? My baby is traveling halfway across the world. I'm going to be there."

"Mom, Maine is in the U.S.," I respond, rolling my eyes.

"I know that, Clem." she snaps back.

It's Sunday night and we've picked up take-out from my favorite Thai restaurant, Chan Dara. Esther, Marina, and Jesus-Marco are coming over for a send-off party.

"They probably won't have Pad Thai on Chebeague Island," I had told Esther, "so I'm going to eat a ton of it tonight."

Pad Thai is my favorite—well, Pad Thai and sushi. I wonder if Chebeague has good sushi. They must if they have great seafood.

Esther brings me a very cute pink cotton scarf. "This is a summer scarf," she insists. "Taylor Swift wears them all the time with tank tops."

"You're right," I say, "I have seen photos of her wearing one of these."

Marina pushes Jesus-Marco toward me. He's holding a small box that looks like he wrapped it. It's entirely covered in tape, and the wrapping paper is orange construction paper that he's colored on.

"Here," he says.

It takes me a while to open up the box, but when I do I find a sticky Hulk figurine inside.

"It was Jesus-Marco's idea," says Marina. "He said Hulk will protect you when you're gone."

Wow. The Hulk is Jesus-Marco's favorite toy in the world; he always carries him around in his back pocket. I'm actually touched and don't know what to say.

"Thank you, Jesus-Marco," I finally manage. "That's really nice of you. I'll take good care of him."

"You better, you stinky frog," he says and sticks out his tongue. Then he skips off toward the TV room.

After a yummy dinner and lots of talk about what Maine will be like, I know that I should probably get a good night's sleep. My flight is at 6 a.m., which means we have to leave the house before 4 a.m. I do not want to be late.

Marina's driving Esther home, so I walk outside with them. Esther gives me a big hug. "I'll miss you," she says. I think that maybe she's starting to cry, so I try to cheer her up by saying, "I'll be back before you know it, and you're going to have a blast with your grandparents!" She nods and climbs into the car.

Then Marina wraps her arms around me tightly. "You be careful. You be strong and smart. God watch over you."

Wow. You'd think I was headed off to Afghanistan or something.

Jesus-Marco refuses to hug me despite Marina's threat to take away his Hulk DVD. I watch them drive down the driveway and wave. I turn around and see Mom leaning in the doorway.

"You ready for tomorrow?" she asks.

"I'm ready." I reply with a smile.

And I really am.

CHAPTER 27

I barely sleep a wink that night. I keep rolling over and looking at my alarm clock. We set it for 4 a.m. because Henry's picking us up at 4:30. My bags are at the door, and I've already showered. At 4:05, I'm up and doing my hair in my bathroom.

Mom peeks in and whispers, "Good morning, Clem. Make sure you leave time for a bagel."

"I can eat it on the way," I reply and continue to work on my hair.

I need to look extra-cute. I've decided on my pink Juicy sweat suit—a comfy choice for flying across the country—and a lime green striped headband, because if Morgan is anything like Miss Lyle, she might appreciate a splash of preppiness. I start to wonder if I should have brought more L.L. Bean-ish clothes, like khakis and wool sweaters. Oh, well. Hopefully, Morgan will welcome a little LA style into her world.

Before I know it, Henry is at the door to load my bags into the trunk. I yell to Mom to hurry up. It's 4:35 and we're supposed to meet Miss Lyle and the other kids at the entrance of the terminal at 5 a.m. sharp.

"Coming! Coming!" she shouts from the other side of the house.

I hop into the back of the limo and realize that it's still pitch dark outside. My mom slides in next to me. She's carrying two bagels and two Vitamin Waters.

"Breakfast to go!" she says.

"So I hear we're headed to LAX, Miss Clementine?" Henry asks, smiling in the rearview mirror.

"Yes, Henry, LAX!" I yell.

When we arrive at the airport, it's surprising to see how busy it is. I would have thought that at 5 a.m. everyone would be sleeping. But the terminals are busy with honking cars pulling up to the curb, taxi cabs, busses, and yelling policemen motioning cars to keep moving. Henry maneuvers the limo to the right and up ahead I see Miss Lyle and Leon standing at the curb. But then I hear Henry mutter, "Oh, no, we got trouble, Ms. Calloway."

"How many?" my mom asks.

"I would say six or seven, Ms. Calloway."

"My God, I can't even take my daughter to the airport? That's really so interesting to them?"

Photographers. Someone must have gotten wind that one of us is traveling. They're obviously in desperate need of some kind of story.

"Great," I say. "If I miss this flight because of those stupid photographers—"

"You're not going to miss this flight, I promise," Mom replies as she peers out the window. "Henry, what do you think?" Mom asks. Her voice sounds a little nervous. I wonder if we should have brought Rocco. Mom never travels without him.

"I think you should stay in the car and I will escort Miss Clementine."

Mom sits back like a balloon that someone's let the air out of. She seems so disappointed.

"It's OK, Mom," I say. "I'll be fine. You know they'll chase us even more if you're with me."

"I know, Clem, but this is something I really wanted to do. I'm your mom. I should be able to get out of the damn car and give you a real send-off."

I want to tell her that I'm used to this. That this is normal to me, that I'm used to doing things without her, that I'll be fine. But it looks to me like she has tears in her eyes, so I decide not to.

We pull up to the curb and the flashes go off immediately. Henry walks around the car and I can hear him yelling, "Out of my way, out of my way!" Finally, I can see the cameras being pushed aside and Henry's face in the window.

Mom wraps her arms around me so tight I think I'll choke. "I love you, Clementine. Be safe. Call me when you get there. You're all I've got."

"OK, OK, I'll be fine. I love you too." I push open the door and let Henry pull me close to him.

I can hear photographers yelling, "Where are you going, Clementine? Are you going to meet your father? Are you going to rehab?"

I'd been taught at a very young age to just keep my eyes down and let Henry or Rocco get me to where I was going. We somehow make it through the crowd of flashes and yelling, and soon I find myself inside the terminal. Apparently, the police stopped the photographers at the door. I look behind me; they're still taking pictures through the glass.

"You OK? Boy, you're popular this morning!" I hear Miss Lyle's voice coming my way. Leon is behind her. He's carrying a backpack and MP3 player.

"I'm fine," I say. "Where's Ebony?"

"Oh, bad news. She decided last night that she couldn't do it. She was homesick before she even packed.

It's probably for the best. We wouldn't want to get her all the way to Maine only to have to fly her home."

I agree, but I was really hoping to have another girl on the trip. I mean, Leon is nice and all, but it would have been nice to have Ebony in Maine with me. Oh, well. I decide not to let it bother me. If she had come with us, we might have had to cut the trip short. That wouldn't have been fair to Morgan and me, and I guess Leon too.

CHAPTER 28

I've never flown anything but first class before. And to be honest, I haven't flown on a commercial plane since I was maybe three. One of the perks of having a rock star mom is the use of private jets. She refuses to buy one, saying that she doesn't like flying enough and doesn't want to be environmentally irresponsible. But when she needs to fly, we always fly on a private jet. There are special companies that rent jets out to people who want privacy when they're flying. Miss Lyle planned everything about our trip, so that's why we're flying on a regular airline. I'm excited to fly in the coach of a plane and, once we're in Maine, ride on a ferryboat. I wonder if the boat will have a pool or planned activities.

As we sit in the terminal, I text Esther that I MHA, miss her already, and Mom that I love her and not to worry. I would text Marina, but she has a pay-by-the-minute cell phone that she can never find. Also, I don't think she knows how to text. For the first time, I feel really grown up.

It's fun to watch all the people getting ready to board the plane. There are tired-looking young parents dragging screaming toddlers behind them and businesspeople on their laptops, looking up only to see if it's time to depart. I see the flight attendants walking down the hallway, chatting and holding coffees, wheeling their bags behind them. I think that would be a fun job for Esther and me, but only if we could always fly on the same plane. Two pilots walk behind the flight attendants. I try to figure out which one is the head pilot and which one is the co-pilot. I'm guessing the older one with the salt-and-pepper hair is the guy in charge. I hope so; the other one looks like he's eighteen and fresh out of pilot school.

Leon is busy on his MP3, and I wonder how his fingers aren't sore. He just keeps pushing away at the buttons, once in a while whispering "Yes!" or "Crap!" Miss Lyle tells him he's not allowed to say crap.

In my carry-on bag, I have a book of poetry, my journal, and my iPod. I'm hoping the poetry book will impress Miss Lyle, and I really do like to read it. It's new, with lots of the writers we learned about in her class. Finally, I hear our row being called, and Miss Lyle says it's time to go.

As we file onto the plane, a flight attendant with a neat black bun greets us in the doorway. "Welcome aboard," she says with a smile.

I smile back and follow Miss Lyle down the aisle. We keep going and going. Are our seats in the back of the plane? Leon's still trying to play his game as he maneuvers down the aisle.

"Put that away, Leon," scolds Miss Lyle.

We make it to our seats, and, yes, we are at the very back of the plane, right in front of the bathrooms. Gross. Who picked these seats anyway? If I start to smell those bathrooms, I am demanding to move.

"Do you know that a plane this big will drop out of the sky like a bowling ball if it stalls?" asks Leon as he adjusts his headgear.

"Shut up, Leon," I say. "Do you know you're more likely to get struck by lightning than to get into a plane accident? Actually, *you* might have a higher chance of that given all the metal in your mouth."

"You guys, we just got on board, can we please get along?" pleads Miss Lyle.

Leon practically pushes me over to grab the aisle seat. He looks up at us and says, "I have to sit near the lavatory. I drank a lot of water."

"Whatever," I reply, "just move your legs so I can get past you."

He lifts up his legs and Miss Lyle and I squeeze into our seats. I sit in the middle so Miss Lyle can look out the window.

We'll be stopping first in Newark, New Jersey. I've been to New York several times but never to Newark. I wonder if it's pretty. I hope we can maybe see it out the window from the airport during our layover. Miss Lyle says we'll have to sit for about two hours in Newark before the next plane takes us to Maine.

Newark—even that sounds amazing.

CHAPTER 29

"**D**id you know that William Carlos Williams was not only a poet, but a pediatrician as well?" Miss Lyle asks when she sees me reading one of his poems in flight.

"You mean he was a doctor?" I ask, stunned. "A kid doctor?"

"Yes, he also delivered babies, they think more than two thousand in the state of New Jersey."

"No way. He must have been so smart. A doctor and an amazing poet. I wish that I had been alive and he were my doctor," I remark. I imagine going for my doctor's appointment and bringing my journal of poems.

We would sit and share our poetry before he gave me my checkup.

"Yeah, that would've been neat, wouldn't it?" she responds with a laugh.

Miss Lyle is so smart. She knows all kinds of neat facts like that. I feel so lucky to be traveling across the country with her.

Leon is no longer playing his Gameboy. Instead, he has his head cranked back. He's fast asleep. He's a very loud breather, probably because of the headgear. I decide I better try to nap too. It's a long flight, over four hours. Plus, I'll probably be up late tonight with Morgan.

CHAPTER 30

When I wake up, Leon is awake, once again intensely playing that stupid electronic game of his. Miss Lyle's sipping hot tea.

"I got you a Coke and some cookies while you were sleeping," she says. "You should eat something."

"Thanks," I reply, still feeling a bit groggy.

Miss Lyle says I will be exhausted tonight because of the time change. They call it jet lag. My mom is always complaining that she's jet lagged, even when she's only traveled from San Fran to LA, where there's no time difference.

"So was it hard saying goodbye to Mom?" asks Miss Lyle as I bite into a chocolate chip cookie.

"No, I'm used to it. She's away all the time."

"Well, I can't imagine you ever really get used to having your mom away. You must miss her a lot."

"It's not so bad," I lie. "What do your parents do?"

"Well," she began, "my dad is a professor of mathematics at a local college. And my mom teaches kindergarten on Chebeague."

I knew it. I picture what her house must be like, white with a little fence out front, right on the ocean. Her parents would be home every night to help her with her homework and tuck her in.

It was like she could read my mind because she looked straight at me and said, "It wasn't always easy. My dad didn't become a professor until I was in high school. Before then, he taught math at a high school that was two hours from our house. And he didn't make that much money. My mom was taking college classes during the day. So we struggled. No Disney vacations for our family. And there were many nights when he would get home long after we were asleep."

It still sounds more normal than my life.

I lean back and am hesitant to ask a certain question, but then I do. "Do you ever regret not going with your boyfriend?"

"Oh, you mean when he was traded?" she asks. She doesn't seem uncomfortable at all.

"Yes, to be, like, a hockey wife," I respond with a smile.

She laughs. "No, I don't. You know, it just wasn't me. I wasn't meant to follow someone else's dream and sit on those cold bleachers every night."

"Yeah, but, did you want to, like, marry him?"

"Part of me did, probably. I mean, I'm at an age when all my friends are getting married. But I think I'll know when the right guy comes along. And he was—how do I put it—kind of controlling."

"What do you mean?"

I can't believe that I'm talking to Miss Lyle about her ex-boyfriend.

This is what it must be like to have a big sister.

"Well, he would get really jealous if I wanted to go out with friends or do anything by myself. You know, Clem, I would just tell you that any guy who is really jealous all the time and doesn't trust you probably is not trustworthy himself."

She looks out the window and sips her tea. I decide not to ask any more about him.

"I heard your mom is giving one-third of her concert profits to UNICEF," she says after a few minutes, a very serious look on her face. "That's a lot of money to give."

"What's UNICEF?" I ask. The name sounded familiar, but I wasn't sure exactly what they did.

"It's a charity that helps children and families all over the world, children who don't have clean water or enough food to eat. It's pretty amazing. And I think what your mom is doing to help them is spectacular."

"Yeah, I guess so." I wish my mom talked to me about things like this. I almost feel like I could learn more about her from magazines sometimes.

All of a sudden, the plane jerks a little.

Leon and I both look anxiously at Miss Lyle.

"Just a little turbulence," she says reassuringly. "We're almost to Newark, so it will probably get a little bumpy as we descend."

The plane jerks again. I peek out of our row to see what the flight attendants are doing. They're laughing in the back, pointing out something in a magazine. Phew. They're not preparing for an emergency landing. If they're OK, we're OK.

I hear a loud ding followed by a deep voice on the loudspeaker.

"Good morning. This is First Officer Chris Jordan from the flight deck. We've put on the fasten seatbelt sign, and we ask that you keep your seatbelts fastened until further notice. Looks like stormy weather in Newark, so we'll be circling until it improves. We'll keep you posted. Meanwhile, please try to stay seated. It may get a little bumpy for a while."

"Yikes, looks like we'll be delayed," says Miss Lyle with a worried look on her face. "I hope we can still make our connecting flight."

Leon leans his head toward me and whispers, "We're so going down in a ball of flames. You better text your goodbyes right now."

"Shut up, Leon. You're not scaring me."

But I am a little scared. You can barely see out the windows because of the dark gray clouds. Every few seconds, it feels like the plane is going to drop.

We circle Newark for over an hour. I desperately have to go to the bathroom, so I squeeze out past Leon, who's now immersed in his four hundred-page book titled *Gargoyles and Wizards*.

"Excuse me, miss. Where are you going?" asks the flight attendant with the tight bun.

"I've got to use the bathroom."

"It can't wait?"

"No."

With an annoyed look on her face, she says, "OK, just hurry. You're not supposed to be up and about."

What am I supposed to do? Wet my pants? Pee in a cup?

I hurry to the bathroom and open the door. The light comes on. It smells disgusting in here, like a sewer combined with lemon cleaning solution. And it's so small. I wonder how some of the really big people on the plane can fit in here.

I carefully make a nest of toilet paper on the seat, then turn around and pull my pants down. As I do, the plane lurches to the left, and I almost fall over. I hover over the toilet, bracing myself so I won't fall.

Suddenly, the door flies open and there stands a man with a mustache and long hair.

I scream.

"Jesus Christ!" he yells. "Why didn't you lock the door?"

"Just shut it!" I cry.

He closes the door and my heart pounds.

Oh, my God!

I'd pulled my pants up—in the middle of peeing. I think I've wet my pants a little. I make sure the door is locked and assess the damage. My underwear and pants are a little wet, so I blot them both with paper towel.

Suddenly, there's a knock on the door.

"Excuse me, miss?" It's that witch of a flight attendant again.

"Yes?" I ask, still trying to clean myself off.

"I'm going to have to ask you to return to your seat now. We are beginning our descent into Newark."

"Just a minute," I yell back.

Why is she chasing me around the plane? Doesn't she have more important things to do?

I hurry as fast as I can, but I feel so gross. I make my way out of the bathroom—and right into Mustache Man. I now notice that he's also covered in tattoos from his neck down to his wrists.

"Sorry, about that," he says. "But you need to lock the bathroom door."

I guess that's his attempt at an apology, so I just respond, "Yeah, I thought I did."

I make my way back to my seat.

"Are you OK?" asks Miss Lyle.

"Fine," I fib. "My zipper was stuck."

"Oh. Well good timing, we're landing. But we've already missed our flight to Maine. We're going to have to see when the next one leaves."

At least I'm going to be able to get off this plane.

"Landing is the most dangerous part of flying," says Leon.

"Leon, just leave me alone, OK? Keep your stupid comments to yourself."

When we finally land, all of the passengers clap.

Why are we clapping?

This has been the worst flight ever.

CHAPTER 31

We find out in Newark that we can catch an express flight to Maine in two hours. That will leave us enough time to have lunch in the food court. I'm starved. We order pizza while Miss Lyle makes phone calls to Maine about our delay.

After she's off the phone, I ask, "Did you call Morgan's dad?"

"You mean Ryan?" she says.

"Yes, Mr. Rich."

"Yes. He said he'd be there with Morgan to pick you up."

"What's he like?"

"I'm not sure. My parents know of him, but never got to know him or Morgan really well. But they said he's supposedly the best lobsterman on the island."

"Wow." I didn't even know that's what he did. So that's why Morgan wrote he traveled a lot.

"Sounds dangerous," I say.

"It is. Especially in the winter and stormy months. I couldn't do it, that's for sure."

"I could," announces Leon as he bites into his pizza.

"Yeah right," I respond. "You weigh, like, forty pounds. You'd be blown overboard within four minutes."

"You're one to talk. You look like a praying mantis."

"You guys, stop it." Miss Lyle has her serious, strict face on. "Just don't talk to each other. How about that?" I know better than to talk back to her.

I take another bite of pizza in hopes of gaining a pound or two before I see Morgan.

CHAPTER 32

I think Miss Lyle is joking when she points out the window at the plane we'll be taking to Maine.

"I've driven in cars bigger than that," I say, and it's true. A Hummer limo is definitely bigger than the plane I'm looking at.

"It's fine," insists Miss Lyle. "It's an express flight. We'll be up and down before you know it."

Leon looks at me and mouths, "We're dead." I just ignore him this time.

As they're calling us to board, Miss Lyle announces, "I don't think we're sitting together this time. But like I said, it's a quick flight."

Well, that's fine with me. A little break from Leon sounds wonderful. As I make my way down the aisle, I look at my boarding pass. I find my seat by the window and smile at Miss Lyle to let her know I'll be fine.

The seat next to me is empty, so maybe I'll get to sprawl out for a while. I buckle my seatbelt and look out the window. The weather's improving. It isn't as dark. It was kind of nice to see rain, though. California can go weeks and weeks without rain. But the minute it rains or gets even a little bit cold, like sixty degrees, everyone gets out their foul-weather gear and boots like they're going to be climbing Mt. Everest in a blizzard. Miss Lyle would laugh at the Los Angeles meteorologists fore-casting code-red storm alerts. She would tell us about storms on the island where she couldn't leave her house for days and the ferries wouldn't run. Now that's a code red.

"Excuse me, I think I'm sitting here."

I look up at the most enormous man I've ever seen staring down at me.

"Oh, sorry." I move my magazine and handbag off of the seat next to mine.

He turns around to put his things in the overhead compartment, and I almost threw up. I can see half of his butt because his pants come down way below his waist. So gross. And hairy.

I have the worst luck.

It takes him forever to get situated, and then he sits down next to me.

"I'm gonna have to put this up." He points to the armrest.

"That's fine," I say quietly.

His body is now spilling over into my seat. I try to inch myself closer and closer to the window. He smells like beef stew. He fiddles around with his bag, the armrest, and his seat. Then he takes his shoes off.

"These monkeys need some air," he chuckles.

He asks if he can stow his shoes in front of my seat because he has so much stuff with him.

"Sure," I reply, trying not to seem overly annoyed.

The smell is almost enough to knock a person over. He pushes the shoes past my face and leans over to tuck them under the seat in front of me.

"You from Maine?" he asks.

"Nope, California."

"Wow, you're a long way from home. I've never been to California. It's not part of my territory. I cover the East Coast down to the Carolinas."

"Oh really, what do you do?" I try my best to sound interested.

"Lighting. You know the exit lights that are on all the time in the hallways of schools or buildings? Up above doorways? That's what I do. I sell those puppies. You always have to exit, right?"

"Yeah, I guess."

I think if I had to pick the most boring job in the universe, it would be selling those exit lights.

"It's a pretty good living. Traveling, schmoozing with clients, fancy dinners. Yeah, life is pretty good."

Well, at least he's happy doing it.

"So what are you doing in Maine? On vacation?" he asks while shuffling through the brochures and emergency cards in front of him.

"Kind of. I'm with my teacher. I have a pen pal there, so I'm going to stay with her for a couple of weeks."

"Cool. Just be careful. I had a few cyber-pals that I went to visit and wish I hadn't, if you know what I mean. Hope you brought warm clothes. I heard it's supposed to get pretty nasty up that way for the next few days."

"I'm all set," I respond.

"Where do you live in California?"

I wish I could just relax and not talk, but he keeps going and going, clearly wanting to chat.

"Los Angeles. Actually, Beverly Hills."

"Well, holy crap—are you one of those celebrity kids? Hey, weren't you in that movie with the pig and the spider?"

"You mean *Charlotte's Web*? No, that was Dakota Fanning."

"Do you know any stars? Hey, do you know Robin Williams? He is my favorite. Now, that man can act. One minute he's flying around as Peter Pan, the next minute he's a psychologist in that movie with the smart, crazy kid. What was the name of that one?"

"*Good Will Hunting.*"

"Yeah, that's it. 'It's not your fault. It's not your fault. It's not your fault.'"

I realize he's quoting a scene from *Good Will Hunting*, and I think for a minute he might cry. He wipes his left eye and says in a whisper, "Gets me every time."

This man is certifiably crazy

As we taxi down the runway, he takes out a headset attached to nothing and announces, "Sweet silence, baby. I put these suckers on any time I wanna tune out my sister's husband. Real loudmouth. That guy never shuts up, if you know what I mean."

He should talk. I fumble for my poetry book and pretend to read.

Twenty minutes into the flight, he takes the earphones off.

"So, really, you know any stars?"

At that point, I estimate we are halfway through our flight. I contemplate lying, but he's kind of a funny man, and I'm curious to know what his reaction will be if I tell him who I know.

"Actually, my mom is kind of a star," I say.

"Shut up! Let me guess. Is your mom Loretta Lynn? No, too old. Hold on, don't tell me. Don't tell me. Cameron Diaz. No, I don't think she has kids—"

"Gray Calloway."

"No way! Run me over with a frickin' snowplow! You're full of it. Are you serious? I am a fan from way back. Are you serious, Gray Calloway?"

"Yes."

He's so excited, it's pretty comical. His eyes are wide and I can tell that he's totally amazed. My smile, however, is short-lived as he quietly breaks out in song.

"And you…are the love…the one that got away…"

He gets louder and louder. I can see Leon peeking over his shoulder at us, pointing and laughing. I scowl back at him.

"The one that got away…oh, the one that got away…" he continues, completely out of key. It's one of Mom's first number one hits, though you can barely recognize it with his singing ability.

"Um, you don't have to do that," I whisper.

But he doesn't hear me. He continues on, singing one song, then another and another.

"Pump up the jam, pump it up…" he yells out.

"That's not my mom's song."

He stops singing. "Are you sure?"

"Yes, I'm sure."

Finally, the pilot announces, "We are beginning our descent into Portland, Maine. The time here is 4:24 p.m., and the weather is sixty-two degrees.

The man shakes his head. "Gray Calloway—so what's it like? Do you have a maid and a limousine and all that?"

"Yeah," I respond, almost feeling badly about it.

"Wow. I got Louise. She comes and cleans every two weeks, but I'm thinking I need to get rid of her. I think she craps up more than she cleans. Plus, I think she steals from my change cup."

"Well, that's good that you have a cleaning lady," I say cheerfully.

"Yeah, well, when you travel like I do, there's not much time for scrubbing toilets, if you know what I mean."

"Do you have a family?" I ask.

"Nope, too busy with my job. And to be honest, just haven't found the right girl yet. Hey, your mom's single, isn't she? How about I give you my number and you give it to her?"

I can't tell if he's serious or not, so I just nervously laugh.

"I'm just kidding. I bet she's got all the celebrity men banging down her door. She's a beauty, your mom."

"Thanks."

I hadn't even noticed that we'd landed. Although I could have done without the singing and the smell, this guy was kind of funny.

"Hey, what's your name?" I ask.

"Roy. Roy Rudebaker. You ever need emergency lighting, you know who to call." He hands me his business card. "Or if you find yourself in Poughkeepsie, look me up. You have fun in Maine. It's gonna be a lot different than Beverly Hills, that's for sure."

"Yeah, I'm hoping for that."

He laughs, puts his shoes back on, and shuffles down the aisle.

"You ready?" asks Miss Lyle.

"Ready," I respond confidently.

CHAPTER 33

Miss Lyle's parents are picking us up at the airport and driving us to the ferry terminal. I can tell that she's excited to see them because she's smiling as she's collecting her things to get off the plane. Or maybe she's just happy to be back in Maine.

As we exit the plane, I pull my cardigan tightly around my body. It's cold here! And the airport seems so small compared to LAX.

"Is this the whole airport?" I ask, looking at the one long building.

"Yup," replies Miss Lyle.

We walk up the steps leading into the terminal and down a long hallway. I see one coffee shop and one gift shop selling a variety of colored sweatshirts with pictures of loons, moose, and lobsters on them. There's a mural on the wall of what looks like a lake, with pine trees, more loons, and another moose drinking from the lake.

"I feel like I just stepped into an L.L. Bean catalog," remarks Leon.

We all laugh at that, and then Miss Lyle yells, "There they are!"

There is a glass wall in front of us, but we can see a man and a woman waving and holding up a big sign that reads "Welcome to Maine, Leon, Clementine, and Ebony…and welcome home Colby!"

Aw, that is so nice. I guess they haven't heard the news about Ebony.

Miss Lyle's parents are exactly as I'd pictured them. Her dad is not a big man, about Miss Lyle's height. He wears khaki pants, of course, and a collared shirt with a green fleece vest over it. He has round tortoiseshell glasses and his gray hair is tousled. He definitely has that professor look going for him. Miss Lyle's mother is adorable, a tiny lady with a brown bob like mine. She's dressed in a navy blue skirt with tiny white anchors all over it, a white shirt, and a bright orange sweater tied over her shoulders.

"Hello! Hello!" Miss Lyle's father shouts. "Welcome to Maine!"

"Mom! Dad!" cries Miss Lyle as she gives big hugs to each of them. "I want you to meet two of my star students. This is Leon, and this is Clementine."

"But aren't you missing one?" her mom asks with a worried expression. "I thought you were bringing home three."

"Yes, Ebony backed out last minute. Thought she'd get a little homesick. Maybe next year. Leon, Clem, these are my parents, Skip and Catherine Lyle."

Leon and I both say, "Hello Mr. and Mrs. Lyle."

"Oh, no," chuckles Mr. Lyle. "You're in Maine now and school's out. We're Skip and Catherine, OK?"

"OK," we both nod.

"Well let's go get your luggage," Catherine says and puts her arm around my shoulders.

I just knew they'd be nice and adorable, like their daughter. We take an escalator downstairs.

"How will we know which luggage belt our bags will be on?" I ask.

I remember that at LAX, you have to find your flight on the screen to figure out where to go collect your luggage.

"Oh, there's only one luggage belt in this airport, and you're looking at it," Skip replies with a laugh.

After a few minutes, the luggage begins to circle around and my red suitcase is one of the first to appear.

"There's mine!" I yell with excitement. It's suddenly becoming very real to me that I'm in Maine, and I'm going to be here for two whole weeks!

"I got it, I got it!" yells Skip. "That bag's bigger than you are, Clementine!"

Soon after, everyone has their bags and we walk out the automatic doors.

Above the doorway, I notice a big sign that reads "Welcome to Maine...the way life should be."

That makes my smile even bigger.

CHAPTER 34

When we get outside, the sky is gray and the air feels almost raw somehow. The weather reminds me of December in Los Angeles. Except here, everyone looks perfectly warm and wears shorts and flip-flops. I want to keep my cardigan on, but I don't want to seem like the wimpy girl from Beverly Hills already.

"Right over here," says Skip. He is walking in front of us, pulling my bag with one arm. He has his other arm around Miss Lyle. They're happily talking back and forth. You can tell that they are close, and, for the first time in a long time, I think about the fact that I will probably never have a dad.

Skip leads us to a white Volvo station wagon with bumper stickers on the back window. One reads "Colby College," and the other "UMaine Black Bears." Skip loads the luggage, and Miss Lyle, Leon, and I hop into the backseat.

"You guys hungry?" asks Catherine, turning around in the front seat to face us. "I brought some apples, granola bars, and water, just in case."

"Water would be great," Miss Lyle says. "Thanks, Mom."

It's funny to hear Miss Lyle call someone Mom.

"I'd love a water," I reply quietly. "Thank you."

"An apple, please," yells Leon in his annoying loud voice.

He proceeds to chomp on the apple in my ear for the next ten minutes as we make our way out of the parking lot.

The first thing I notice is all of the trees. And that the airport just doesn't seem super-busy like LAX. There aren't many cars on the road leaving the airport.

"Well, this is it, guys!" Miss Lyle beams at us. "Are you excited?"

"Definitely," I reply.

Leon just nods because his mouth is filled with apple. He's taken off his headgear and put it in his lap. Disgusting.

Soon we're traveling on a road called 95. Miss Lyle tells us that Maine does not have any freeways and that this is pretty much the biggest road.

"Where are the billboards?" asks Leon. I hadn't even noticed.

"Maine doesn't have any," Miss Lyle replies. "The law doesn't allow them, actually."

Wow. That makes so much sense, because then you can just drive along and enjoy the trees without being bombarded every fifty yards by advertisements and reminders to stay off drugs.

The drive to the ferry will take us about twenty minutes, but Miss Lyle says it will be a very pretty drive. What sounds like country music is playing on the radio.

"You guys like Lyle Lovett?" Skip yells from the front. "We were at his concert just last Thursday. Amazing."

I haven't heard of Lyle Lovett, but I smile to let them know that the music is fine.

Catherine turns around again and grins at me. "Now, your mom is a musician, correct?"

"Yes, her name is Gray Calloway. She sings."

"OK, now what type of music does she sing?" she asks, seeming genuinely interested.

"Well, I guess you'd call it pop rock," I reply.

"Pop what?" asks Skip.

"Dad, how can you teach college kids and not know Gray Calloway?" asks Miss Lyle, laughing.

"I teach linear equations. I don't really spend much time discussing rock stars with my students."

"Wow, well that must be very exciting," Catherine says to me, pointing out the exit to her husband.

"I know where I'm going," he says. He turns up the radio and sings along.

CHAPTER 35

The drive to the ferry is beautiful. We get off 95 and drive through a town called Falmouth.

"Is this the entire town?" asks Leon.

"Well, this is the main street, where pretty much all of the stores are," replies Miss Lyle.

"But there is also a library and the schools. You can't see them from here," adds Skip. He sounds like he's defending the little town. But he doesn't need to. I think it's really pretty.

"There's Shaw's," Catherine points out. "That's one of the places where folks from Chebeague Island stock up on groceries."

"How do they carry them all back to the island?" I ask.

"Well, it's tricky. Some people bring wagons and some have them delivered."

After we drive for a while, we take a right onto a small road that winds through the trees for miles. The houses range in size; some are big and beautiful and others are small and cozy-looking. And I also see a few trailers, which seem so tiny. I can't imagine living in such a small space.

Skip turns down the music and says, "Once we get over this bridge, we'll be on Cousin's Island, and then it's time for your ferry ride."

The bridge is long and narrow. The water on both sides looks gray and choppy, not the kind of ocean you'd want to swim in.

"Is it always like that, the water?" I ask.

"It's a little stormy today," Miss Lyle says with a reassuring smile. "It will calm down. Once the sun comes out, you'll see how lovely it is."

"Well, I brought a thermal, solar-heat-activated wetsuit," comments Leon. "I'll be swimming like a fish, storm or no storm."

Catherine turns around, a stern look on her face. "You need to be really careful in these waters. There are strong riptides that can carry even the strongest of swimmers away. And it's true, the water is cold, even in the summer. Before you know it, your legs are too numb to swim. So never swim alone, even with a wetsuit on, OK?"

I smile and nod, and Leon nods too.

"We're here!" shouts Miss Lyle. We drive down a hill, and there in front of us is the ocean. We see a dock with a big wooden boat next to it. The boat's painted white and red.

"Does that take us to the ferry?" I ask.

The Lyles chuckle simultaneously. Skip answers, "That is the ferry. I'm going to drop you guys off here and park the car up at the lot."

We get our things out of the back and walk down the dock to a little hut.

"Is this structure sturdy?" asks Leon.

"You're fine," replies Catherine.

"We can wait in here if you'd like," suggests Miss Lyle. She pointed to the bench inside the hut.

"No thanks," I say, "I would rather wait out here."

I am beyond excited. I peer out through the fog and can't believe that I'm just minutes away from meeting my new best friend in Maine.

It's weird, but I feel like I know her so well already.

CHAPTER 36

I feel badly as Skip carries most of our bags down the long boardwalk that leads to the ferry, but he doesn't seem to mind.

"Looks like we just made it!" he yells.

The red and white boat is called *The Islander*. I notice that there are orange seats at the top of the boat, but I know the weather probably isn't nice enough to sit up there today. It's sprinkling now, and it seems like the rain is coming in sideways. I'm hoping the rain doesn't make my hair look awful before seeing Morgan.

We walk down a ramp that leads us onboard the ferry.

"Hey, there," says a boy who looks like he's maybe eighteen. He's wearing a yellow rain coat and rain pants with a blue baseball cap with a big red B on the front.

We all smile as we walk past him.

"Hey, Mr. and Mrs. Lyle, how are you?" the boy says with sparkling blue eyes. He buzzes around the inside of the ferry and looks like he's getting everything ready to go.

"Are you the captain?" asks Leon.

"No, I'm the deckhand. Name's Wyatt. You all headed to the island for a visit?"

"Yes," replies Leon. "For two weeks."

"Aw, you're in for a real treat."

As we walk through the door, Skip says, "That Wyatt is a great kid. Goes to UMaine and does this in the summer. He prepares the boat for launching and docking and collects the tickets."

UMaine. That sounds fantastic. Maybe Morgan, Esther and I will end up there together. We would be roommates all four years, join the same sorority, eventually graduate, and maybe move back to Beverly Hills together. Perfect.

I look around and notice that there are not many other passengers on the ferry. There's an older white-haired couple in matching red fleece jackets with a big yellow dog. I've never seen so much fleece in my life.

And there is a young mom with her daughter, who looks like she's three or four. They have a big cart filled with groceries. They must have made a trip to Shaw's.

I suddenly feel a vibration underneath me as the huge boat starts up. The deckhand is now outside, and I can see him untying the ropes that secured us to the dock.

Slowly, the boat begins to move out into the harbor. I can hear seagulls squawking. I wonder if they're the same kind of seagulls as in California, the ones that basically attack you if you try to eat anything at the beach.

"I wish it wasn't so foggy," says Miss Lyle disappointedly, "it's usually such a gorgeous trip. You can't see anything today."

It's true. You really can't see anything. I wonder how the captain can even see where we're going.

"You guys tired?" yells Skip from the seat behind us.

"I'm OK," I reply.

I am a little tired, but too excited to even think about sleeping.

Leon didn't hear Skip because he's back to playing his Gameboy. I decide that I'd better let Mom know that I've arrived safely, so I hunt through my big carry-on bag for my cell phone. I pull it out and immediately notice "No Service" on the screen.

"You'll have to make phone calls when you get to Morgan's house, Clem. Cell phones don't work very well out here," says Miss Lyle.

I feel the boat slowing down, which probably means we're almost there. I try desperately to see anything at all out the window, but it's just too foggy. I imagine Morgan and her father standing on shore. She's probably wearing an extra-fabulous outfit to greet me, and maybe we'll be going out to dinner at a restaurant on the island. I know to look for a girl my age with dark, curly hair. I brought my flat iron because Morgan had mentioned in one of her letters that she sometimes wished that she didn't have curls. We will definitely have to have a spa/makeover night.

The big boat engine becomes louder, and it almost feels like the captain has put the boat in reverse. I look out and see that we're pulling up close to another dock. The deckhand jumps onto the dock and quickly ties up the boat.

"Here we are!" Miss Lyle says, her eyes wide with excitement. "Can you believe it? Leon, I'm taking that game thing away. No more video games while you're here, OK?"

"What? Not at all?" whines Leon.

"Nope, you can take a two-week vacation from electronics."

Miss Lyle takes his Gameboy and tucks it in her purse. I think Leon is going to cry.

"And Clem, even if you get service on your phone, I want you to take a break from texting and making too many phone calls home, OK?"

I agree. I know Esther will be waiting for me when I get back. I wonder if she's missing me already.

Everyone files out of the boat. My stomach is in knots. I just hope that Morgan will like me.

Once we're off the boat, we walk up another ramp and I can see a group of people waiting at the top, waving.

CHAPTER 37

The rain is steadier now, and I am glad I pulled my raincoat out of my luggage on the ferry. My hood is up, but I am debating whether to put it down when I see Morgan. I wonder which person she is—the fog makes it difficult to see faces.

"Hello! Hello!" I hear a man's voice bellowing as we step off of the ramp and onto land.

"Welcome to Chebeague!" another voice yells, this time a woman.

I scan the crowd. There are six people there, two men, a woman, two boys, and a girl. But the girl looks like she's young, maybe six or seven. And she has blond hair. That's definitely not Morgan, unless she's really small and has recently dyed and straightened her hair.

"You must be Leon," says the woman. She has brown hair tied in a loose ponytail and is wearing a blue raincoat and navy blue boots with green whales on them. "We are so happy you're here!"

Leon walks to her with a half-smile and the woman's husband shoves one of the boys toward him. "This is Seth. Seth, say hi to your pen pal!"

Leon and Seth shake hands awkwardly shake hands awkwardly. "This is Lucille, Seth's little sister," Seth's mom says.

I'm devastated. Where's Morgan? Did she forget what time I was arriving?

Suddenly, the other man, who seems gigantic in his yellow raincoat and big black boots, walks toward me. He has a scruffy face, like he can't decide whether to grow a beard. His hair is a mess. It's dark, but I can see lots of gray in it too.

"You must be Clementine," he says and holds out his hand. "I've heard all about you."

Confused, I murmur, "Yes, I'm Clementine. Hi."

"Morgan, Morgan, get over here. She's finally here and you're hiding," the man says with a smile.

A boy with dark, curly hair steps out from behind him. He's my height but has big cheeks, and I can tell that he's a little overweight. He smiles a wide smile and, to my astonishment, wraps his arms around me.

"Well, that's more like it," says the man, who's clearly his father.

"I'm Morgan," he says after he's pulled away. "I'm so happy you're finally here."

In a panic, I look around for Miss Lyle, but she's busy talking to Leon's pen pal family.

"We're going to have so much fun," the boy says. "And look, I wore this for you." He unzips his raincoat to show me a gray Mickey Mouse T-shirt, which is clearly two sizes too small for him. "See, it says Disneyland!"

I'm still in a state of shock. This can't be right. My pen pal is a girl. Her name is Morgan. She's not an overweight, curly-haired boy in a Mickey Mouse T-shirt.

"Disneyland, the one in California," he continues, obviously waiting for my reaction.

"Oh, yeah," I mutter.

Finally, Miss Lyle makes her way over to the three of us. She looks at me; I can tell that she's also surprised.

"Oh, so you must be Morgan?" she asks.

"Yes, nice to meet you," he responds and holds out his hand.

"How you doing, Clem?" Miss Lyle asks me. "Do you want to have a quick talk before we all head out in different directions?"

I'm sure she can see it written all over my face. I'm devastated. It wasn't supposed to happen like this. She takes my hand and guides me near the water.

"Are you OK?" she asks.

"Um, I'm just really surprised," I reply, trying to fight back my tears. "I thought Morgan was a girl."

"So did I, Clem. I guess we just assumed. The name and all. Just like poetry, life can be unpredictable." Miss Lyle has her hands on my arms, and I can tell that she knows how upset I am. "What do you want to do? I don't want you in an uncomfortable situation."

"I don't know," I respond.

"I think you should give them a chance, Clem. I've heard that they're pretty amazing people, and I think Morgan would be really disappointed if you backed out. But at the same time, I'm not going to force you to stay with them if you don't want to."

I look at my feet. I look at the water. I look at the ferry already on its way back to the mainland. I look back at the big man in yellow and the boy picking up rocks and inspecting them.

"Can I try it?" I ask, my voice shaking.

"Of course. You stay a couple days and then you let me know what you want to do. You could always come stay at our house," she assures me.

I can do this. Don't cry. Don't cry. Ten days. It's nothing.

I think of Natalia Steins visiting her crazy grand-mother three times a year at the institution with pad-ded walls.

Yes, I can do this.

We slowly walk back to the big man and Morgan. The man gets down on one knee and says gently, "You know what? I forgot to introduce myself. My name's Ryan, Ryan Rich. We're so happy you're here. We've got lots of fun things planned, Morgan and me."

I force a smile and nod. Miss Lyle squeezes my shoul-der, smiles, and winks. And before I know it, I'm climb-ing into an old red truck that makes Marina's car look like a brand new Porsche.

CHAPTER 38

I'm sandwiched in the middle of Ryan and Morgan as we travel up a dirt road. "That there is the Chebeague Island Inn, the yellow building. Over a hundred years old," Ryan says.

Even in the fog, it's beautiful. Yellow with a huge screened in front porch, and a big yard that goes right down to the ocean.

"You hungry? You must be after that long flight. Morgan and I made some chowder that I think you'll like. Rich family recipe," Ryan says with a smile.

"Yeah, thanks," I respond quietly.

I'm really not in the mood to chat. I'm tired and still shocked that I'm not going to have a new BFF in Maine.

"I think the weather is supposed to get better in the next day or two. And then I can show you the rope swing. Have you ever been on a rope swing?" Morgan asks.

"No," I reply shortly, hoping to send a message that I just need some quiet time. But it doesn't work.

"It's so much fun! It's up on a cliff, and if you pull it way back, you feel like you're flying before you hit the water," Morgan says. He uses his hand to demonstrate a person flying up and then down, apparently into water. He even adds sound effects at the end. I dodge the flying spit when he yells, "Spppplllashhhhhh!"

"Wow," I say in a very unenthused voice.

Perhaps sensing my annoyance, Ryan leans over and says, "Hey pal, Clem's probably really tired after her long trip. Let's give her a few minutes to take in the sights, OK?"

Morgan nods but continues to stare at me the entire trip home. The wipers are on high now, and I think they might fly off the windshield. I can't see a thing, let alone sightsee.

A car and a truck pass and Ryan and Morgan wave at each one.

"Island custom," Morgan explains, "you gotta wave when someone passes you by."

"Oh," I mutter.

I can just imagine if I had to wave to everyone who passed me by in LA.

"There's Doughty's Market, pretty much sells anything you need, and quite a few things you don't," Ryan chuckles.

"Will Doughty is a friend of mine," exclaims Morgan.

I feel the truck turn to the right then come to a stop. Ryan shuts off the engine, but it continues to sputter repeatedly before cutting out with a loud boom.

"This truck has seen better days, that's for sure," laughs Ryan. "I've had her since I was seventeen. Can you believe that? Seventeen."

I can believe it. It doesn't have seatbelts, it has the kind of windows you roll up yourself, and the entire floor is covered in newspapers, coffee cups, and napkins.

"Well, home sweet home," Ryan says. "We ready to make a run for it?"

My luggage is in the back of the truck. Ryan put a big blue tarp over it back at the dock and I hope my stuff isn't soaked.

"You guys run in and I'll grab Clementine's bags, OK?" Ryan says.

Morgan looks outside, then back at me. "You ready?"

I nod, a bit hesitantly as I'm not sure where I'll be running to.

Morgan makes several attempts to open the truck door before it finally gives and we spill out onto the dirt driveway.

"This way!" he yells, and I follow him to the little yellow house, through the garage, and up the steps that lead into a tiny kitchen. Once inside, he looks at me with his brown eyes wide and exclaims, "Boy, it's crazy out there! It usually only gets like this during hurricane season!"

Hasn't he heard the news? Clementine Calloway is in town—and wherever she goes, bad luck is sure to follow.

CHAPTER 39

Though very neat, this is definitely the tiniest house I have ever been in. The kitchen has a stove, but it's not just the kind you cook on; it also keeps the place warm, as well. It isn't on now, but I can tell it's well-used given all the soot on the bricks around it.

The kitchen floor is covered in linoleum meant to look like tiny bricks. I notice some holes in it near the refrigerator. The cupboards are yellow, and over the small sink there's a window. I can't see anything out of it because of the downpour.

"Come on, Clementine, I'll give you the tour." Morgan pulls my arm toward the next room.

I'm not sure if I'm seeing things or still groggy from my flight, but as we enter, I swear that the entire house is on a downhill slope. It's higher in the kitchen, lower here.

I assume this is the living room. Its brown walls look like wood, but I'm not sure it's real. The floor's covered in a light beige carpet that's clearly seen better days. There's a couch with brightly colored flowers and a big chair next to it that's still reclined. I immediately notice that one wall is covered in photographs. I walk over to take a look; Morgan follows and stands next to me.

"That's me when I was a baby." He points to a photo of Ryan with a woman who must be his mother, holding a baby proudly. The baby looks like a newborn.

"Your mom's really pretty," I comment, thinking maybe I should have said "was really pretty."

"Yeah, everyone says that."

His mom's hair was this light reddish-gold color and her eyes were bright blue, not at all like Morgan's brown ones.

There are lots more pictures. Ryan standing on a boat with Morgan by his side. A bunch of school pictures of Morgan, sitting with that fake clenched smile we've all made at one time or another. Given his wardrobe selections for photo day, I think he can desperately use a makeover.

"Well, here's all your stuff. Boy, you've got a lot of stuff," laughs Ryan from the garage door.

"Girls have a lot of stuff, Dad," Morgan yells back. I notice that they're both really loud talkers, and, given the small size of the house, they really don't need to be.

"Let me show you where your room is," Morgan says as he jumps up onto the flowered couch, then bounces off. I follow him down a very narrow and dark hallway.

"Here it is!" he yells excitedly.

"Um, is this your room?" I ask, looking around at all the boy stuff on the walls and shelves.

"Yeah, but while you're here, I'm on the porch. It's screened-in. And if it gets cold, I'll just go onto the couch. I like it out there."

Morgan completely changes the subject. "Look, Clementine, this is the book of poetry I was telling you about. The poets are all from New England."

"Wow." I try to sound a bit more lively. "I'll have to look through it some time."

"And this is the trophy I won last year for the spelling bee. Second place. Next year, I plan on winning it."

"That's great. I'm not that good at spelling."

"Mannequin," he says flatly.

"What?" I ask.

"Spell mannequin."

"I don't really want to."

"Just try. Mann-e-quin," he enunciates.

I'm getting annoyed again, but I try to hold it together. "I told you, I'm not a good speller."

"Mannequin. M-A-N-N-E-Q-U-I-N. Mannequin. That's the word that got me out last year," he says solemnly.

"Well, you definitely won't get it wrong next year," I say, trying to seem interested.

"Exactly," he affirms. "Do you want to read some of my poetry in my journal?"

"You know, I'm pretty tired, and I should probably call my mother to let her know I'm here," I say quietly.

Morgan's room looks a lot like the living room. Wood on the walls and brown carpet on the floor. His bed is made neatly, with a colorful quilt on top that looks handmade. Next to his bed, I notice a framed photo of Morgan and his mom. He is older in it; it was probably taken just a couple of years ago. They're on a beach and she's hugging him. They're both smiling at the camera.

"Can I use your phone?" I ask.

"Sure, this way," he replies as he skips out of the room. Even though he's my age, he acts younger than me, not at all like most of the boys at my school.

I follow him to the kitchen. "There's the phone!" Morgan points to the wall.

The phone had a cord and looks like one of those old-fashioned ones from long ago.

"Thanks," I reply and dial my mother's cell.

"Hi, Clem." I immediately recognize Hali's voice. "How's Maine?"

"Fine. Is my mother there?" I ask.

"You're as chipper as ever. Mom is on stage rehearsing. Can I have her call you back? She's been worried sick."

If she's worried sick, why can't she just take my call?

"Sure, can you take down this number? My cell doesn't work here."

"Bummer," she responds. "I have it. It rang up on the phone when you called. Talk to you soon! Have fun!"

I hang up and see Morgan lingering in the kitchen, probably just wanting to listen to my phone call. Ryan's put my bags in Morgan's room and is now taking off his wet raincoat.

"You ready for some chowder?" he asks brightly.

"Sure," I say with a half-smile. It does smell really good, but I don't have much of an appetite.

CHAPTER 40

The chowder is delicious. I wish Mom could taste it. She loves soup of any kind, and this one is creamy and chock full of clams and potatoes.

"Is it OK, Clementine?" asks Ryan as he hands me a basket filled with warm rolls.

"It's really good, thanks," I say, my mouth full.

"The Rich family secret ingredient is corn and a big, chopped-up onion," he says with a wink.

I smile and scoop another spoonful into my mouth. Morgan's tucked a napkin into his shirt and is smiling as he eats.

"So, Clementine, what's your impression of Maine so far? A lot different than LA, I'm sure," Ryan says with a laugh. I can tell he is trying hard to make me feel comfortable.

"A lot different, from what I've seen so far. A lot less crowded. Smaller streets," I reply.

"That's for sure," he laughs. "You've got those free-ways. Man, I don't think I could handle it, all those people."

"I guess you just get used to it," I reply as I butter my roll.

"I guess Miss Lyle got used to it. She's a Maine girl, but I guess she has adjusted to life in Los Angeles," Ryan says and then takes a sip of his water.

"Yeah, she's great," I respond.

"My dad has a crush on my teacher," announces Morgan.

"Morgan, don't be ridiculous," says Ryan sternly.

"Dad, Miss White? You get all crazy-acting at parent-teacher conferences. It's so obvious," laughs Morgan.

"You're crazy," Ryan replies adamantly. "I don't act any different with her than any of your other teachers."

I'm a little embarrassed because I can tell Ryan is uncomfortable. I try to change the subject.

"How many kids are in your class, Morgan?" I ask brightly.

"I think I told you in my letter. Seven."

"Oh yeah, I forgot."

I'm still having a hard time connecting the pen pal letters with the boy sitting across from me. How could I have missed the clues? Did he purposely deceive me?

"Did you save room for dessert, Clementine?" asks Ryan. "We bought some whoopie pies."

"What are whoopie pies?" I ask, almost laughing.

"Oh, my gosh," says Morgan, "you've never had a whoopie pie?"

"Well, they are kind of a Maine thing," replies Ryan, standing up and taking my empty bowl with him. "Well, you're in for a treat, then. You might have to bring a few home to your friends. Might start a new Beverly Hills trend."

Morgan gets up from the table and walks over to the large paper bag on the counter. He puts his hand in and says, "This is a whoopie pie." He pulls out something that kind of looks like a gigantic Oreo because it's brown on the outside with what looks like white frosting sandwiched in the middle.

"Is that, like, cake on the outside?" I ask, still perplexed.

"Yeah, I guess so. Just try it!" says Morgan excitedly.

I unwrap my whoopie pie. It isn't the kind of pie you cut up. I take a bite and can't hide my smile, it's that good. The cake doesn't taste like any chocolate cake I've ever had before. It's moist, and the white filling is light and doesn't taste like frosting, although it's sweet. The whoopie pie is delicious, and I wonder why we don't have these in Beverly Hills. Mr. Parker would make a fortune if he sold these on the playground.

"See," begins Ryan, "the key to a superb whoopie pie is the cake on the outside. If it's too dry, it just doesn't work. It's got to be a nice, moist cake. Anne down on Dover Street makes these for the gift shop at the boat-yard, and I've never found a better one yet."

Despite the fact that I've just eaten the best dessert creation I've ever tasted, I'm still depressed that this is my first day in Maine and my pen pal is not going to be my lifelong BFF. I'm supposed to be staying up late sharing my innermost secrets with Morgan—the *girl*—not the Morgan who keeps staring at me with his big brown eyes from across the table.

"Is it OK if I take a shower?" I ask Ryan as he washes the dishes.

"Of course, I should have offered. Morgan, show her where the towels are. You need a washcloth? I think we've got some somewhere. Let me think—"

"No, I'm fine," I reply. "Just the towel would be great."

"Follow me," says Morgan, who once again skips down the hall. I think about the last time I skipped; I can't even remember it.

I follow Morgan to a very small, very green bathroom. The floor's lime green linoleum and there's a green rug on the floor, the same rug that covers the toilet seat lid.

"Here's a towel," says Morgan, "and be careful with the hot water. It's a little unpredictable."

"Thanks," I say.

Morgan points to a Barbie doll on the toilet. She's wearing a green knitted dress that wraps over a roll of toilet paper.

"My grandma made that," Morgan tells me. "She lives in South Paris."

"Wow, that's neat. I'd love to visit France," I reply, feeling awkward standing in the bathroom with him.

"No, Paris, Maine," he replies with a laugh.

"Oh, right. Well, I'm going to shower now."

I quietly close the door and for a minute just stand there, not believing the situation I've gotten myself into. Basically, I only have nine days left now. That's not so bad. I pull back the shower curtain and turn on the hot water, then the cold. Maybe I'll feel better after a hot shower.

I step in and relish my time alone. Five minutes into it, though, the water suddenly turns ice cold, and I almost jump out. Instead, I arch my back and scream.

"You OK in there?" bellows Ryan from the hallway.

Embarrassed, I yell back, "Fine! Just a little cold water!"

"Yeah, it's our well. Kind of unpredictable," he answers.

Yes, I heard. Nine days. Nine days.

After my very unrelaxing shower, I dry off using a towel that feels like tree bark and change into my pink pajamas. I tiptoe down the hallway and peek into the room with the television. They are sitting together in a large recliner chair. Ryan has one arm around Morgan. I'm smiling, watching the two of them.

"You want to watch some tube with us?" Ryan calls from the living room.

"No, thank you," I call back. "I'm really tired. I think I'll head to bed."

"You sure? We're watching *Nancy Grace*. But I can change it if you want."

I almost turn around. I don't know anyone else except Marina who loves watching *Nancy Grace*. I think about watching it with her, and how angry she gets at the bad guys Nancy always talks about. I wonder what she's doing right now. Probably chasing Jesus Marco around. I wonder if she's missing me yet.

"No thanks, I'll see you in the morning." I head back down the hallway.

"Good night," I hear both Morgan and Ryan yell together.

"Good night," I yell back.

But it's true. I really am exhausted, and the thought of small-talking about California and my life there makes my head hurt. I know that if I just go to sleep, I'll wake up in the morning and see Miss Lyle. After all, we have group activities planned for the whole week. So it's not like I'll be on my own the whole time.

I pull back the quilt on Morgan's bed. Maybe his grandmother in South Paris made it. It has all different colors and what looks like Raggedy Ann and Andy dolls on it. On the walls are various paintings and drawings that look like Morgan had created them. They're mostly of the ocean and boats, with one portrait that looks like his mother. I also see two Chebeague Island School certificates on the wall, one for perfect attendance and the other for second place in the spelling bee.

Mannequin. M-A-N-N-E-Q-U-I-N. Mannequin.

I slip under the quilt and pull it up over me. I can hear Ryan and Morgan's voices in the living room.

"Oh, he is guilty, no doubt about it," says Ryan.

"Yeah, but if you listen to Nancy, I think she thinks the sister did it," replies Morgan.

"No, Nancy rips into everyone, guilty or not. That's just Nancy," adds Ryan.

I almost laugh, but I'm too tired.

Before I know it, I'm asleep in Maine.

CHAPTER 41

"**G**ood morning!" Morgan yells from the doorway. *OK, this is not a dream. I really am in a slanty house with a pen pal who is not a girl.*

I look at my watch.

"Um, Morgan, it's 6 a.m."

"Oh, that's California time. You're in Maine now. It's nine. Dad's making his famous blueberry pancakes."

"OK, OK, give me a few minutes to wake up."

Morgan disappears and I imagine him skipping down the hallway.

My head feels like it's been squashed by a truck, I'm so tired. So this is what jet lag feels like. I suddenly remember that Miss Lyle said we'd be meeting at noon for a hike, so I quickly get out of bed and put on a sweatshirt. The house does smell good; because it's so small, you can smell breakfast even at the other end of the house. That certainly isn't the case at my house. We have an intercom system that Marina uses to tell me to come down for meals.

I slide into my Hello Kitty slippers. I always feel a bit babyish in them, but Esther got them for me and assures me that Hello Kitty is not just for kids. She has a ton of Hello Kitty stuff. I already miss her, and I can't wait to see how she'll react when I tell her that Morgan was actually a boy. And then I think about Mom. I always like to imagine her at home, curled up on the couch with a magazine. But I know she's not there because well, she hardly ever is.

I make my way to the kitchen and see that it's sunny out.

"Good morning, Clementine. How'd you sleep?" Ryan asks. He's standing over the stove with a spatula in one hand.

"Great, thanks," I say, still feeling groggy.

"Do you like blueberry pancakes? We picked the blueberries out back yesterday," Morgan says while digging through the refrigerator. He pulls out a container of orange juice and pours three glassfuls.

"Yes, sounds great."

I'm starved. Miss Lyle told me the Maine air would make me hungry. Maybe she was right. The pancakes smell so good, and I know in an hour or so I'll be with Miss Lyle—this puts me in better spirits. Granted, I'll also have to hang out with Leon, but at this point, I don't mind. I wonder how he's doing without his Gameboy. At least he has a boy his age to hang out with. I have Morgan—this boy who acts like he's seven with severe bedhead and who's still wearing the too-tight Disneyland T-shirt from yesterday.

I sit down at the table and pick up the newspaper in front of me. I have to smile at the headline: Moose and Dog Become Pals. There's a picture of a moose with a dog sitting right next to it. In Los Angeles, the headlines are always about someone getting killed, a shooting, or a robbery.

"Here you go. Eat up. We've got plenty." Ryan hands me my plate. The top pancake is shaped like a heart. I look over at Morgan's plate and he has one too.

"The heart thing, it's what my wife, Morgan's mom, used to do." Ryan doesn't look up from his cooking. "She never made pancakes without making some into hearts, so I just keep the tradition going."

I look at Morgan for his reaction, but he's busy digging into his pancakes.

"That's nice," I reply. I think about how hard it must have been to have a mom one day and not the next. Morgan and his dad seem so close.

The pancakes are thick, filled with blueberries, and piping hot. I reach for the syrup and the phone rings. Morgan races to grab it.

"Hello?"

I watch his face go from happy to gloomy, and I know in an instant that something's wrong.

"Wow, that stinks," he says. "Yeah, we'll be fine. Thanks." Then he hangs up.

"You're not going to believe it," he begins, climbing back into his chair. "Miss Lyle went for a run on the trails this morning and is at the hospital. She slipped, and they think she broke her ankle."

"Oh, no, on her first day back? Where is she? Maine Med?" asks Ryan.

"Yeah, that was her dad. He said they'd call when they knew more."

My heart sinks. First, because I feel sorry for Miss Lyle. She must be in a lot of pain. And second, because this means I'm stuck with Morgan and won't be hiking with Miss Lyle.

"Well, Clementine, looks like you're going to have to hang out with us for a few days," Ryan says as he sits down with his plate of pancakes.

"I can take you to the rope swing today!" yells Morgan in a voice that's much too loud for early in the morning.

A rope swing actually sounded like fun. And if a beach was involved, even better.

CHAPTER 42

After breakfast, Morgan instructs me on what I should put in my backpack for the day. I throw on a bathing suit and sunblock and fill up my water bottle. I emerge from the bedroom in my new white cover-up, little high heels, and Lilly shades that will be perfect for the beach. Morgan takes one look at me and laughs.

"You can't wear that! We're hiking through the woods to get there."

Slightly embarrassed, I reply, "Well, how am I supposed to know?"

"You're right, I should have told you. Do you have anything a little more, well, casual?"

I dig through my suitcase and find shorts and a tank top. I trade my heels for sneakers. The house seems like it's getting really hot. I'm sweating already and wonder if there's any air-conditioning.

When I return to the living room, Morgan says, "Let's go. We're meeting one of my friends there."

Thank God.

I was hoping it wouldn't be just the two of us.

In the daylight, I get a better look at the house. It's very small and looks like it could use a good paint job. We walk down the dirt driveway and cross a street.

"How far is the beach?" I ask.

"Well, it's not technically a beach," Morgan says. "It's about a fifteen-minute hike."

I follow him as he heads into the woods. I can see that there's a trail, and I start feeling like an explorer in one of my history books. Almost immediately, however, I can barely see in front of me because of the little flies buzzing around my face. I swat at them, then I realize that they're also landing on my legs and arms. I don't want to complain because Morgan is just strolling along like nothing's happening. Why are they just attacking me?

Suddenly, one of the bugs flies into my mouth. I cough because I swear I can feel it fluttering in the back of my throat. I make a choking sound. Morgan stops and turns around.

"Oh, you've met our black flies. They're really bad this time of year, especially in the woods where it's damp."

He pulls a bottle of spray from his backpack as I try to clear my throat.

"Close your eyes and hold your breath," he cautions.

I put my hands over my face, and he sprays me from head to toe.

"OK, you're all set," he says and returns the bottle to his backpack.

"Thanks."

It's really hot, and humid, too. I guess I didn't realize that Maine would get this hot. It seemed so, well, north. We hike and hike for what seems like an hour, but when we emerge from the woods, it's really only been fifteen minutes. In California, it's only eight in the morning.

Thinking that we're going to a beach, I'm surprised to see a small pool of water that looks more like a stream. There are rocks all around it, and the water is flowing from a little waterfall a distance away. It's really pretty.

"Hey, Morgan! I'm up here!" I hear a girl's voice calling from somewhere above us.

I look up to my left and see a girl, probably about my age, in jean shorts and a blue T-shirt, standing on the bank.

"Hey!" Morgan calls back. "How's the water?"

"I don't know! Not allowed to go in unless a friend is with me!"

The blond-haired girl tosses her glasses onto a towel next to her, grabs a rope hanging from a tree, walks backward with it, kicks up her feet, and swings into the air. She screams as she drops into the water below. I'm nervous at first because she doesn't come up right away, but then she splashes out of the water like a seal, laughing.

"The water's great! You've got to try it!"

She's close enough now that I can see she has freckles, lots of them. They seem like they are everywhere. She takes a breath and disappears underwater again before surfacing right in front of us.

"Meet Georgia," says Morgan, kicking water in her direction.

"Oh, like the state," I say. I feel somewhat out of place.

"Yeah, my parents are from there originally. And you must be Clementine, like the fruit?"

"Yes, the fruit," I respond.

"Come on, follow me." Morgan points to a small trail leading up the bank to where Georgia had jumped off.

I'm nervous; I'm not sure I want to leap in the water yet. When we get to the top, I see Georgia's stuff in the grass. On top of her blue towel is a book titled *The Life and Poetry of Longfellow.*

"Morgan says you like poetry. Are you a Longfellow fan?" I didn't realize that Georgia had already made her way out of the water and was on top of the bank with us.

"Um, yeah, he's great," I respond.

Which one is Longfellow? I can't remember.

Georgia picks up her towel and wraps it around her. Her clothes are drenched, and water's still rolling down her freckly face.

"What's your favorite Longfellow poem?" she asks, putting on her glasses.

"Hmm, that's a tough one," I say. "He's got so many."

I feel like I'm taking a quiz right now. I don't want to sound like I'm just some dumb girl from Beverly Hills.

I have never seen anyone pull off freckles so well. She looks like one of those girls in the J.Crew catalogs. I can tell already that she probably is the type of girl that would never wear make-up, or cutlets or hair extensions, for that matter. She's just naturally pretty.

I watch Morgan wrestling to take off his tight T-shirt and feel embarrassed for him. Why doesn't he just wear it? His arms are over his head, and his belly hangs out over his elastic-waist shorts.

"Got it!" he yells as the shirt comes off and lands on the ground next to him.

"You going to jump, Clementine?" asks Georgia, her towel still wrapped around her like a dress.

"I don't know, I'm kind of tired," I stall.

I can't think of any excuse other than being tired. I just don't feel like stripping down to my tankini and jumping off of a cliff into ice cold water. And I don't have any sort of a tan yet, so I know I'll look way too skinny and white.

"Tired?" she responds with a laugh. "Just one jump in the water and you will not be tired anymore. I promise."

"Yeah, well, maybe next time."

I pull my towel out of my backpack, lay it down next to me, sit down, and pretend to check my cell phone.

"Clementine! You have to jump! You said in your letters that you couldn't wait to jump into the Maine water," Morgan says with a slight whine that bugs me even more.

"I'm just not into it today."

I'm not sure why I'm feeling so out of place. I mean, everyone is really nice. But I just don't want to jump into the water and make a fool of myself.

Morgan is smiling ear to ear as he walks over to the edge and yells, "Jackknife!" He jumps into the water holding one of his knees. The big splash almost reaches me, and I'm a good ten feet up.

"Don't you swim?" asks Georgia.

Here we go. Why can't they understand that I just don't want to?

"Yes, I swim. I have a pool at my house." I may have rolled my eyes, but I'm not sure.

"Well, this is more fun than a swimming pool. Trust me. Just try one jump. You'll love it," she pleads.

"Fine. One jump, but then I'm going to hang and get some sun."

"Suit yourself!"

Morgan swims in the water below as I take off my white cover-up. It's strange that I'm the only one in an actual bathing suit. It's my new favorite, a Shoshanna with cherries all over it.

I make my way to the edge and peer over. It's a long way down, but I remind myself that the high dive at school is probably the same height, and I've dived off of that countless times.

"You probably just want to jump in your first time. I wouldn't try anything fancy. Also, make sure you jump out at an arc because there's jagged rock at the base," Georgia cautions.

I know that I have to do an amazing dive. I can't just jump. That would be like a baby jump.

"I'll be fine," I reply.

I decide I'll do a stag leap and show them that I really am athletic. After all, they only get to swim three months out of the year; I'm able to swim 24-7.

Just don't look down. Take a deep breath.

"Come on. Just jump already! Show us what you got!" yells Morgan.

Deep breath. Jump out and bend front knee like Coach Evans has shown me a million times. But make sure to jump out away from the rocks.

I count down from five in my head. And then I jump.

The next thing I know, I'm underwater and my lungs are killing me. I've jumped out too far and landed smack on my back, which has clearly knocked the wind out of me. The water is like ice. I frantically make my way to the surface and gasp.

Morgan is at my side. "Are you OK? I've never seen anyone hit the water so hard!"

My new Shoshanna is so far up my butt I don't know how I'm going to pull it out.

Morgan helps me to the bank, where I grab on for dear life, I try my best to calm myself down. Georgia's there too, rubbing my back, telling me to take deep breaths.

Finally, I can sit up. Morgan wraps my towel around me.

"That was awful!" I say, almost crying.

"Well, usually when you jump in, your feet go in first. You were horizontal when you hit the water," Georgia says.

"Well, that's the last time I try that." I wipe a tear away from my eye.

My back is burning from where it hit the water, and I still can't believe how cold the water is. How can anyone find that enjoyable? I leave them there and go gather my things. I just want so much to be normal, to fit in. But so far, just like at the school dance, I'm managing to make a total fool out of myself.

CHAPTER 43

The first half of the walk home is silent. I'm still a little shaken up, and I really don't feel like talking about it. But Morgan is one of those kids who cannot go ten seconds without hearing his own voice, so if he's not talking, he's singing or whistling or making crazy noises that he insists are birdcalls. But, of course, he has to start in with his questions again.

"So are you homesick yet?" he asks, kicking a rock out of his way.

"No."

"Do you miss Jesus-Marco?" he asks with a laugh.

I forgot that I had told him about Marina and Jesus-Marco in one of my letters.

"No."

Am I homesick? How can I be homesick? Do I really miss a home where I'm alone most of the time?

"Tomorrow night's the concert I was telling you about. I think you'll really like the singer."

This perks me up a little. I've been looking forward to seeing live Maine music.

"Do you ever wish that you had two parents?" Morgan asks.

How could he ask me something so personal?

"Excuse me?"

"Oh, sorry. We had written about that to each other— the fact that we both just have one parent. I didn't mean to upset you."

"No. It's fine. I mean, having one parent. It's fine." But I know my response is a lie. I'd give anything to have a dad, or at least still have my grandfather. Dads are the guys that make you feel beautiful even when the whole world thinks you're not.

"I kind of wish I had two parents," says Morgan as he stops to inspect a small bug on a leaf. "I wouldn't mind if my dad asked out Miss White. She's a real nice teacher on the island. Then my dad wouldn't be alone."

"He's not alone. He has you."

"Yeah, but, you know, someone to go on dates with and to cook for him sometimes. And to do his laundry and roll his socks into balls and make *him* heart-shaped pancakes the way my mom used to.

"I never think about it," I lie again. I sometimes think that if my mom had a husband or at least a boyfriend, he would say to her, "Gray, you need to slow down a little…spend more time with Clementine."

"Wow, you're lucky. I wish I never thought about it. But I guess it's different, because you've never met your father. So you can't really miss someone you don't know."

"Well I'd rather have it that way. I guess I'm the lucky one."

When this comes out, I instantly know that I shouldn't have said it.

Morgan stops in his tracks and turns around. He looks me straight in the eye.

"I wouldn't trade the eight years that I had with my mom for anything on earth. Yeah, I miss her and it hurts, but I got to have her for eight years, and I'm lucky for that."

I look down at my shoes. What is wrong with me?

"Sorry," I whisper. And I truly am.

Morgan turns around and keeps walking.

"You know, Clementine, you're a lot different in your letters than you are in real life," he says after a few minutes.

"So are you," I say.

I want to tell him that I think he's lucky for having all those years with his mom. And he's lucky that his dad still makes him heart shaped pancakes, like she did. But I don't, and we walk the rest of the way in silence.

CHAPTER 44

When we return home, Ryan's still down at the boat so Morgan suggests we have lunch and walk down to visit him. He makes us peanut butter and jelly sandwiches to go, wrapping each one in a paper towel. I change out of my bathing suit and into a T-shirt and miniskirt. We walk down a dirt road, and I can see the ocean. It looks beautiful today and I can hear seagulls in the distance. I can also see the Inn, the big yellow building that looks like a house. I'm thinking about how Georgia must think I'm a total freak. I wonder if she's at home right now telling her parents about my horrible dive.

I follow Morgan out the door and we head down toward the water where all the boats are.

I haven't done this much walking since our school trip to Knott's Berry Farm, the big amusement park in California. If your group happened to get a lazy teacher or a substitute, you were golden because they basically let you go free for the day, as long as you met up with them at a certain point. We got Mr. Mike, a substitute who had clearly stayed up way too late the night before because he slept on the bus the entire way there and back. When we arrived, he said, "Yo, I'm gonna go catch a little shut-eye. Just stay together and meet me at one at the giant jam jar."

I wonder if Morgan has ever been to an amusement park. I want to ask him, but I doubt he wants to talk to me right now.

We finally reach the marina. There are six or seven very long docks jutting out into the water. On each side of the docks, there are probably about fifteen boats. A few of them look nice, like the kinds at the Hamptons. Our next door neighbor there is the president of the largest bank in America and has a boat the size of a house. Sometimes he'll have big parties on the boat and invite us. I think he has a secret crush on Mom, even though he's married with teen twin daughters, Margaret and Mary Kate. Every time we get on the boat, he says to Mom, "Gray, let me take you on a private tour." She always looks at me and rolls her eyes. "Oh, thanks," she tells him, "I've already been on a tour—a few times."

As we walk down the dock, I can see Ryan on one of the boats. It's not as big as I expected. There are lots of big box type things that look like cages with nets in them. Ryan is busy stacking them.

"Hey, Dad!" yells Morgan.

"Hey, big guy!" Ryan yells back. "You guys done with the rope swing already?"

"Yep, we only jumped a couple of times," Morgan replies, hopping onto the boat. I hope and pray he doesn't tell Ryan about my embarrassing jumping mishap.

"Hey, Clementine, how was it? You score a ten on your diving?" Ryan laughs as he continues stacking traps.

"Not exactly," I respond quietly.

"Come aboard, my lady. If I had known you were coming, I would have cleaned the place up." Ryan holds out his hand. I take it and hop on deck.

"Her name is *Kristin Alexandra*," Ryan says. "Welcome aboard."

"Who's Kristin Alexandra?" I ask.

"That's my mom and the name of our boat," responds Morgan proudly.

Kristin Alexandra. That's a pretty name.

"You guys want to go for a ride?" Ryan asks. "Show Clementine the shoreline?"

Morgan and I shrug and nod. We're not very convincing.

"What's up with you two? Have a fight or something?" he asks with a laugh, but we are both silent. The engine of the boat is now running and we are backing up. Morgan is helping by pushing us away from the dock.

"Hey Dad, can I steer?" asks Morgan, perking up.

"Not until we get out a little bit. You know that. And then maybe we'll let Clementine steer. How about that?"

I give Ryan a little smile. And despite the fact that Ryan and Morgan are not at all what I expected, I find myself just wishing that they would like me and think I'm amazing.

Ryan lifts up a seat and pulls out two life vests. He tosses them to Morgan and me.

"Aw, Dad, you know I can swim if I need to," Morgan protests.

"Oh, really?" Ryan says. "What if the boat flips and you're knocked unconscious? Can you swim then?"

I immediately put my life vest on without saying a word.

The boat tour is beautiful. Ryan shows me where he keeps some of his traps, which are the rectangular cage things that are all over the boat. They're marked by buoys, and Ryan has special gear that raises them so he can check for lobsters. He pulled up one trap and pulled out a lobster with his bare hand.

"You want to hold one, Clementine?" It has big claws and it's squirming all around. It's not bright red like I thought it would be. It's actually a deep maroon, with black spots. Ryan tells me that it only turns bright red when it's cooked.

"No way!" I say, and I'm laughing now. Those claws look like they could pinch really hard!

I ask Ryan why he wanted to become a lobsterman.

"There's nothing like it," he responds as he looks out at the sea. "My daddy worked all his life in a cubicle smaller than this boat, with no windows. I just knew I couldn't be cooped up like that. One day after I had graduated from high school, I saw an advertisement for a deckhand on Casco Bay. I knew in my heart that it was my calling. I learned from a lobsterman all I needed to know, and then as soon as I had saved up enough money, I bought my own boat. It's not easy. And every year it seems like someone wants to see the lobstering industry crumble. But we lobstermen look out for each other. No, it's not easy—but it's the life I chose, and I wouldn't trade it for the world."

"Hey, look Clem, a harbor seal," Morgan says, pointing to the playful animal by the side of the boat.

Pretty cool.

CHAPTER 45

When we pull back into the harbor, the sun's beginning to set.

"Look, red sun at night," says Morgan, pointing to the sun. It's beautiful, hanging above the horizon like a bright red ball of fire.

"That's an old sailors' saying," Ryan explains. "'Red sun in the morning, sailors take warning. Red sun at night, sailors delight.' It's supposed to mean that tomorrow will be a good weather day."

"Oh," I reply with a nod. But I'm not really listening. I'm thinking about getting back so I can call Mom and tell her about my day. When we return, it's dark. Ryan cooks burgers on the grill and I dial my mom's cell number. After the beep, I leave a message. "Hi, Mom. It's me, Clementine. Just thought I would check in. I'm doing okay. I miss you." I hang up and run to the bathroom, quietly shutting and locking the door behind me.

Tears are streaming down my face. Why can't she be there just once? Just once when I need her, why can't she pick up the phone? I sit down on the bathroom floor with my face in my hands. After a few minutes, Morgan is tapping at the door.

"Clementine?" he says, almost whispering.

"Yes?" I ask, wiping my eyes and cheeks.

"You OK in there? Supper's ready."

"Yes, be right there," I say.

What is wrong with me? Here I am in Maine, where I wanted to be. It's beautiful here and Morgan and Ryan are so nice to me. Why am I sitting on a bathroom floor crying? Is there anywhere on earth where I fit in...where I truly belong?

"Hey, Grandpa," I whisper. "If you're listening, can you help me out? I need you. I'm feeling so alone. I just want someone to tell me everything's going to be okay. Grandpa...please tell me everthing's going to be okay."

A breeze blows in threw the window and I can smell the barbecue. It smells really good. I stand up and examine myself in the mirror. My eyes are a little red, but not too bad. I open the door and find them both sitting outside at a picnic table. Burgers, corn on the cob, potato salad. And even a plate of whoopie pies. That makes me smile.

"You get in touch with your mom, Clem?" asks Ryan, handing me a paper plate.

"No, not yet." I respond.

"Gosh, I'm sure she's missing you," says Ryan. And I wonder if he's doing what Esther's mom always does. Reassuring me that my mom misses me, that she really does love me.

CHAPTER 46

The next morning, we get a surprise knock at the door. Morgan opens it and there stands Miss Lyle, looking more beautiful than I've ever seen her. She has on a white sundress and her hair is down. And she is on crutches. I immediately run to her and give her a big hug.

"Oh, Clementine. So good to see you! I'm so sorry about my silly accident. This is not how I planned our trip." She looks at me, and I can tell that she feels terribly about how things have turned out.

"It's fine," I say and smile. "I'm just glad you're OK."

"Hey, how would you and Morgan like to head to the beach with me today?"

"Are you sure you can go to the beach?" I ask.

"Yup. They say it's just a really bad sprain. Just can't do any swimming today."

Morgan and I pack a bag and Ryan tells us that if we need anything, he'll be on the boat. Miss Lyle's dad is parked at the end of Ryan's driveway, and he gives me a big wave as I get closer to the car.

"Hi Clementine! Hop in! We all ready for some beach time?"

Morgan hops in next to me. He introduces himself to Skip, and the four of us are off to the beach. And for the first time, since my arrival, I'm all warm inside. And I smile.

"Oh, wait!" I yell. "Could I just run in and grab something?"

"Absolutely. We'll wait right here," says Skip with a big smile.

Ryan is still outside talking to Skip and Miss Lyle so I sprint into the kitchen looking behind me to make sure I'm not being followed. I open up the refrigerator and scan the shelves.

Lemon. Lemon. Lemon. There has to be lemon in here somewhere.

I open up one of the drawers. Bingo! A big, bright yellow lemon. My mom had told me that when she was a teenager, she and her friends used to squeeze lemon juice into their hair before going to the beach. She said it gave her blond highlights before she could afford to go to a salon.

Brilliant! I will go back to Los Angeles with golden high-lights and a tan! My mom has always said no to chemical changes to my hair, but lemons are totally natural.

I quickly find a knife, cut the lemon in half and race to the bathroom. I squeeze half of the lemon all over the front of my hair until I can't get any more juice to come out of it. Then I do the same with the other half. I brush my hair back into a messy bun, toss the lemon into the trash and race back out the door to the car.

"All set!" I say cheerfully.

There isn't a cloud in the sky as we descend down a long hill that takes us to the marina.

"I thought we were going to a beach," I comment.

"We are. The beach we're going to is on a small island called Little Chebeague. It's like no beach you've gone to before; I can bet you that," says Skip with a wink.

We soon board a small white boat that Skip says is called a Boston Whaler. We all help Miss Lyle get into the boat. I'm so nervous that she might hurt herself. But soon she is seated in the back, smiling at me.

I smile back.

"Hey, Miss Lyle, where's Leon? Isn't he coming with us?" I ask.

"Leon's family took him into town to look at some historic buildings."

"Well, I'm glad I got the beach trip," I yell over the hum of the boat engine.

"Me too, Clem. But Leon will have fun, I'm sure. He's kind of a history buff."

Morgan is standing right next to Skip. I can tell how comfortable Morgan is on a boat. He knows exactly what to do and when. At one point, Skip even has Morgan drive while he takes a picture of Miss Lyle and me.

Within ten minutes, Skip yells out, "There she is! Isn't she a beauty?"

He is pointing at the small island directly in front of us. It has a long strip of sand and then lots of trees behind the beach. A few boats are bobbing in the water in front of the beach, and I can see about eight or nine people sitting in beach chairs on the sand. They are now waving, and Skip gives a big wave back. We maneuver our boat in between two other boats. Skip turns off the engine and finds the anchor that is attached to a long red rope. "Watch your heads!" he yells as he tosses it overboard.

He takes off his shirt and is wearing navy blue shorts with red lobsters all over them. I try to imagine Coach Evans wearing those at school. The kids would totally make fun of him.

"Well, I don't know about you guys, but I'm going in!" And with that he hops over the boat and into the water.

Morgan takes off his shirt and sits on the side of the boat for a few seconds before disappearing into the water.

"Is it cold?" I ask.

Morgan is treading water now and yells, "No! It's great! Totally refreshing."

Refreshing. That always means ice cold.

I take my clothes off and set them down next to Miss Lyle. "Do you want me to stay with you, Miss Lyle?" I ask. I feel badly leaving her here all alone.

"Oh, you go, Clem. Have fun! I brought a book I've been meaning to read. Go and have fun!"

I make my way to the side of the boat, sit on the edge for a few seconds, and then push off. I almost scream when I hit the water because it is absolutely freezing! Skip and Morgan laugh.

"Oh my gosh!" I yell. "How can you guys swim in this? It feels like ice!"

I don't wait for an answer. I am swimming as fast as I can toward shore. Morgan and Skip follow me and soon we are sitting on the warm sand, dripping wet.

"So this island's pretty magical, Clem," begins Skip as he is wiping water off his brow. "I'm going to find you a bucket, because you're gonna want to do some collecting here."

"Collecting? What will I collect?" I don't want to sound like a total girl and say that I'm not really into picking up sea creatures.

"Little Chebeague is known for its sea glass. Some are even shaped like hearts. Colby has a whole jar of heart shaped sea glass in her bedroom at home. It's amazing how Mother Nature can take an old, stinky chard of glass and turn it into something so beautiful." And with that, he holds up a turquoise blue piece of glass that looks smooth and perfect. He hands it to me. It is beautiful, so cool and smooth. I decide that I can collect a whole bunch and give them to Esther, Marina, and Mom when I get back home.

Skip goes off and asks one of the couples on the beach if we can borrow a bucket and returns with a big red one.

"Do you mind if I go with you, Clementine?" asks Morgan, seeming a little shy.

"Sure. Why not?" I ask and begin walking. Skip stays behind and plops himself down on the sand next to the other people on the beach.

I find my first piece of sea glass within minutes. It's bright green and shinier than the one that Skip had given me. "That's a pretty one," says Morgan.

"Hey, can I ask you a question, Clementine?" Morgan asks three steps behind me.

"Sure," I say, hoping it's not something too personal.

"Is it hard having a mom who's so famous?"

Part of me wants to just give my standard response when people ask me this question. That it's great and I get to travel all over the world and meet celebrities like Taylor Swift and Justin Beiber. And I live in a pretty amazing house and have body guards and limousine drivers. But I stop, and I turn around and give him my honest answer.

"It's not easy. My mom is hardly ever home, and when she's home she doesn't like to keep still. She can't sit down and watch a movie with me. She always has to be doing something. She's on the phone, on the computer or meeting with people. I just wish that she was just there more, not just at home but really there. Does that make sense?"

"Yes, that must be really hard."

I start to get a lump in my throat and feel tears welling up in my eyes. I decide to change the subject.

"Isn't it hard to live way out here, with no malls or stuff to do? Doesn't it get really boring? You and your dad must get on each others' nerves out here with nothing to do." I'm hoping he tells me that he is just as sad as me, that his relationship with his dad is not as perfect as it seems. Because I'm realizing that I'm envious. Envious of their closeness and the time they get to spend together.

"It's not so bad," he says, looking out at the sea. "Sure, someday I know I'll want off this island, at least for a little while. But the people are so great. Hard working and loyal, you know? My dad and I couldn't have gotten through losing my mom if it weren't for our island friends and neighbors. And Dad, well, he's my dad. We fight just like anyone else, but he's my dad. I guess after my mom died, I learned that we don't have our parents forever. We really don't. So maybe my dad's not perfect, but he's my dad."

"Hey Clem, can I ask you one more question?" asks Morgan, staring at my head.

"Yes," I answer, suddenly feeling self conscious.

"Why is your hair turning orange?"

Oh no. Oh no. Orange? Mom said that lemon juice gave her gold highlights, not orange!

I cover the top of my head with my hand and try not to freak out.

"Um, sometimes my hair changes color in the sun. It's really weird."

"Really? I've never heard of that. That's crazy," he says, his eyes wide open inspecting my hair.

What am I going to do? Oh no. Orange hair. This is just what I need.

I race ahead of Morgan and find four more pieces of sea glass. I then head back toward the boat and yell, "All done!"

Skip and Morgan follow as I swim out toward the boat. It is somewhat difficult, because I am dragging a bucket behind me. When I finally make it to the boat, Miss Lyle directs me to the ladder in the back.

"Find lots of sea glass, Clem?" asks Miss Lyle.

Please don't notice my hair. Please don't notice.

My hair is wet which prevents anyone else from noticing for now. But as we get going, the wind is blowing through my hair and I know it's only a matter of time before it's completely orange again.

Suddenly Morgan yells, "Hey, Miss Lyle! Did you know Clementine's hair changes color in the sun? Show her, Clem!"

Thank you, Morgan. I feel like choking him.

Miss Lyle looks at me with concern. "Clem, look at me."

Reluctantly, I turn my head and face Miss Lyle. She gasps.

"Um, Clem, what's going on with your hair?"

"Well, my mom told me that she and her friends used to put lemon juice in their hair at the beach to give it gold highlights. I kind of put a little lemon juice in it before we left."

"Oh my God, Clem! Your mother's going to kill me!" Miss Lyle is using her fingers to look at each strand of hair. "This is not good, Clem."

It feels like I can't go one day without having some sort of disaster in my life. I think Miss Lyle senses that I'm getting upset because she puts her arm around me and whispers, "It's not so bad, actually. Now that I'm looking at it more closely, it's not so bad. And the more sun it gets, it will probably get blonder. It's probably at an in between stage right now, you know?"

I nod my head but don't say a word because I'm afraid that I'll cry. Again.

CHAPTER 47

I spend what seems like forever in the bathroom mirror, trying to part my hair in a way that hides the rust colored chunks in the front. I shake my head and sigh.

Oh well, at least it's an outside concert and it will be dark.

I spray a little bit of Coco Chanel on each wrist, pack up my clutch, and walk down the hallway. The guys are sitting in the living room, and I immediately notice that I'm definitely more dressed up than the two of them. Ryan's wearing jeans and a long- sleeved T-shirt, and Morgan has on khaki shorts with a black fleece. At least he isn't wearing the Mickey Mouse T-shirt. He actually looks somewhat normal.

"Wow, Clementine, you're all dressed up," Ryan says as he stands up.

"Yeah, well, I just thought since it's a concert—" I mumble.

"Oh, no, I don't mean it in a bad way," Ryan says. "You look great! We ready to go?"

Morgan yells, "Ready!" and skips out the door.

I'm happy that I have my shrug because it's freezing! It feels like winter in California as we head down the windy road in the beat-up, rusty truck. Ryan has the windows down and the radio blasting.

"This is probably my favorite song of all time," he comments, bobbing his head up and down.

He turns down the radio slightly and asks, "Do you know who this is, Clementine?"

I shake my head, and I really don't care.

"This is the Grateful Dead. Now, this band knew how to write a song. Man, Jerry Garcia—he was the lead singer—was unbelievable. I saw them play a few times. Best concerts ever."

I've heard of the Grateful Dead. I know that some people are so into it that they totally dress like hippies and basically worship the band. I don't think the group's together anymore, though.

"Were you, like, a Deadhead?" I ask.

"Well, I'm not sure if I was a true Deadhead. I didn't sell all my stuff and follow them around the country or anything. But I did meet Kristin at one of their shows in Maine. She was sitting on a blanket with some friends. Her hair was a mess, but beautiful. I found out later that she was trying to grow dreadlocks, and, boy, I thought that was the coolest thing ever. I walked right up to her and said, 'Hi, I'm Ryan. This song playing, "Sugar Magnolia," this is going to be our song.' She just laughed, but I was right. 'Sugar Magnolia' was—is—our song."

He smiles and turns up the music. He and Morgan continue to sing.

"These singers now, they just don't write songs like they used to. They don't mean anything. Songs used to be like poetry, they meant something," says Ryan.

And then he remembers that he's talking to a pop star's daughter. He pretends to bang his head with his fist.

"But not your mama, Clementine. I haven't really listened to her music much, but people tell me she's got soul, not like the others."

People should really know that I could care less if they like my mom's music or not. It pays the bills. And it takes her away from me a lot. So either way's fine with me. I just nod my head in agreement.

We're the only car on the road, which is puzzling because you'd think there'd be a lot more traffic with a live show in town.

We pull over in front of a small, white house. I wonder if we're picking someone else up, but Ryan turns the engine off and pulls the keys out of the ignition.

"We're here!" yells Morgan and jumps out of the truck.

There are lots of cars parked in the driveway and probably seven or so on the street.

"Oh, so this isn't like a concert, concert," I say quietly, unsure if I should have said that out loud.

"Well, it's live music. Not sure what a guy with a guitar has to do to call his playing a concert," replies Ryan. "But you will love Bud Sanders. He's amazing. I don't know how he hasn't become famous yet."

I follow them as they walk around the house to the backyard. There are probably thirty or so people, most of them facing the man who is strumming on a guitar and singing. Bud Sanders has a gigantic gray beard and long hair in a low ponytail, and he's wearing a baseball cap backwards. He's dressed in a plaid flannel-looking shirt, jeans, and big work boots. Ryan is crazy if he thinks this guy would ever become famous. He looks like he has fleas.

People sit on blankets and some even have blankets around their shoulders. They're swaying and singing along to another song that I've never heard before.

I know immediately that this is going to be a long night.

I scan the crowd for Miss Lyle but only find Leon. He's sitting up front, near the singer on a blanket. He's wearing a baseball cap with the letter B on it and a huge cream-colored sweater that looks like someone let him borrow it.

"Hey Morgan, what's the B on the baseball caps stand for?"

"The Boston Red Sox who are THE best baseball team in the world!" he says, almost yelling with excitement.

Leon's sitting next to the boy who picked him up at the ferry. They whisper and laugh and Leon looks like he's really happy. I decide not to go over to him; I'd probably just be a big downer, the way I'm feeling.

"Hi, Morgan. Hi, Clementine."

I turn to see Georgia standing right next to Morgan. She has her hair in braids, which, surprisingly, doesn't make her look babyish. She looks pretty in her jeans, long-sleeved T-shirt, and black fleece vest.

"Hi," I try to look away, hoping she doesn't notice my orange hair.

"You look pretty tonight, Clementine," she says with a smile.

"Thanks," I reply. "You do, too."

"Bud's really great. I love this song," she says with a smile. "You guys want to grab a seat up front?"

Before I can answer, she and Morgan are both singing at the top of their lungs.

"I'm going to take a look around. I'll meet you guys in a bit," I reply.

"Are you sure? Well, come sit with us later, OK?" she says, her eyes bright from the light of the fire.

"Yeah, sure."

I leave them standing there and disappear into the crowd of people.

CHAPTER 48

I find a seat next to the house, far back from where Bud, Morgan, Georgia, and Leon are sitting. I just want some alone time. I wish I could call or text Esther. She would know how to get the orange out of my hair.

I had called my mom before the concert. It had been a quick phone call. She was really busy and I could barely hear her. I could only hear Hali in the background, telling her she needed to get off the phone. I didn't tell her that my hair was orange, or that I was kind of missing her, but maybe feeling more angry at her for not being more like Ryan. I knew she didn't have time for it. She would have said, "Not now, Clementine. I don't have time for the drama."

I can see Ryan. He's talking to a pretty woman about his age with long black hair. She's dressed in khakis and a sweater, a giveaway that she most likely lives on the island. I wonder if she's the teacher Morgan mentioned, the one Ryan supposedly has a crush on.

"Hey, you here by yourself?"

I turn my head and realize that there's a group of older, maybe even high school-aged, kids looking at me.

"Um, no, well kind of," I yell, hoping they can hear me.

A boy, a really cute boy, with gold-ish hair and big blue eyes is smiling at me. He walks my way. My heart beats faster. I look around to make sure he'd been actually talking to me.

"I'm Brady," he says, holding out his hand as he sits down on the grass next to me. "Let me guess. You're not from here."

"How did you know that?" I ask, still startled by the fact that this older, hot boy is actually talking to me.

"The miniskirt, I guess. You don't see many miniskirts around here. And, I don't know. You just have that look about you, like you're lost or something. And the hair. Not too many people do the punk colors in their hair here. Where are you from?"

"California," I respond, turning my head to hide the orange from him.

"No way! I love California. Some of my favorite surf-ing spots are there. Newport Beach? You can't beat it."

"Yeah, I live in Los Angeles. Beverly Hills, actually."

"I knew it! You are so out of place here. I'm from Connecticut. My dad makes us come here in the sum-mer on the weekends. It kind of blows. But it's his attempt to expose us to life in the country or something like that. Do you like it here?"

"It's okay, I guess."

"Hey, you need to hang out with my crew. We're all from somewhere else. Mostly Boston and Connecticut. You hang with us and you'll get through the days just fine. Hey, guys, come sit over here."

Brady motions to his friends, and, before I know it, I'm surrounded by two girls and two other boys. All of them are wearing clothes that you would see in LA. The girls are both wearing really tight jeans with boots, and one has a cute sparkly purple scarf wrapped around her neck. The other's wearing a white hoodie with "Hoochie Girl" on the back of it. I laugh and think of Esther's mom calling girls who wear cutlets hoochies.

"This is so lame," says the girl in the hoochie sweat-shirt. "I wish I were back in Boston."

"Me too," replies the other, taking out her phone. "I am so done with having no cell phone service. Seriously, no bars? Ridiculous."

"Hey, how about we blow out of here?" says Brady. "Oh wait," he laughs, "we don't even know your name."

"Clementine. Clementine Calloway."

"Shut up! You are not!" says the girl with the cell phone.

"What? Why is that a big deal?" Brady asks.

"Hello? Clementine Calloway—as in Gray Calloway's daughter? Don't you read *Celeb Weekly*?"

"No, actually, I don't. Are you really Gray Calloway's daughter?"

"Um, yeah. I am."

I know immediately that they're totally impressed because the girls become my instant BFF's. They're by my side, asking me about LA, the boys, my school, and all about Mom. I answer, trying not to sound like I'm bragging.

"What's the nightlife like there?" asks the girl in the hoodie. She tells me her name is Sloane.

"Oh, it's amazing," I say, wondering what she's talking about. Dances, maybe? Or sleepovers?

"So cool. You must hang out with celebs all the time, like with your mom and stuff."

Sloane's so impressed, I can tell we'll hit it off. Even though she's older, I feel an instant bond. She's so different than Morgan and Georgia, more like my friends in LA.

"Yeah, sometimes," I answer.

I figure I'll let them ask me more questions, rather than tell them all about my friends whose parents are celebrities. They would freak if they knew that Maxwell Bryant's son is my friend. I'll spring that one on them later.

"So let's blow this clambake," says Brady, brushing a piece of his golden-blond hair away from his eyes. "You in?" He's looking straight at me.

"Um, I can't really leave here," I say. "I'm kind of with other people. I don't think they'd let me go."

I tell them all about my pen pal mishap, and how I'm completely miserable.

"Oh, then you've got to sneak out," says Sloane. "We'll just come get you tonight. Like, at midnight." They all nod their heads in agreement.

"Which house is it?" asks Brady. I try my best to explain where Morgan lives, and Brady seems to recognize the street. "OK, then it's set. Midnight."

"Bye, Clem! See you later!" Sloane gives me a big hug and a kiss on each cheek, and then they're all gone.

And I'm left wondering how I'm going to pull this off.

CHAPTER 49

The Bud Sanders concert seems endless, but eventually I make my way to the front to sit with Georgia and Morgan. They're swaying back and forth, singing along to the music. I feel so out of place and just wish it would be over already. I think Leon sees me, but he's ignoring me, and that's fine.

At the end of the night, Bud yells, "I'll see you all here again next week. Don't miss it—the Wailers are opening for me! Thanks for coming out tonight!"

Everybody claps and stands to gather their things.

"Bye, Clementine. Maybe we could try the rope swing again tomorrow," says Georgia as she folds up the blanket.

"Um, never," I reply shortly.

"Oh, she'll go again," says Morgan.

"No, I really won't."

"You ready guys?" Ryan has found us in the crowd. The woman with the dark hair stands next to him.

"Hi, Miss White!" chime Morgan and Georgia.

"Hi! How's your summer, you two?"

She's beautiful and almost looks like she's from another country. Her skin is tanned and she has big dark eyes. I can see why Ryan would like her.

"Good," Georgia and Morgan say simultaneously.

"And this must be Clementine. I've heard so much about you. Morgan has been so excited about your visit to Maine. Are you having fun?"

I nod and force a smile. I'm happy when Ryan says good-bye to her and leads the way back to the truck. I don't even bother saying good-bye to Georgia, but I see her leave, holding the hand of a blond-haired toddler who looks just like her. It must be Ethel, her little sister.

Ryan starts up the truck but doesn't blast the music, which means he will probably want to talk. Maybe I'll pretend I'm asleep.

"You like Bud, Clementine?" he asks as he maneuvers the truck out onto the road.

"Yeah, he was great," I reply.

"He also writes. He published a book of poetry a while back. I think we have it somewhere at home. My wife was a big reader. I think she would have read every book under the sun if she had the chance." Ryan smiles.

I look over and Morgan's already asleep, unless he's faking so he doesn't have to talk. But I doubt it. Morgan loves to talk.

"Sometimes I would just sit next to Kristin and watch her," Ryan goes on. "I'd watch her just read or fold laundry. She got real sick at the end so she was mostly in bed. But I just loved sitting next to her, studying every laugh line and freckle, taking in the flecks in her blue eyes. Sometimes she'd say, 'You know, Ryan, I can just tell you're sitting there thinking. Thinking too much about the future, about what's going to happen when I'm not here, about Morgan and how he'll be.' She'd get so mad when I thought and worried too much."

"Well, I would think that would be normal," I say, "given the circumstances."

I'm pretty impressed with my response. I think it sounds very grown up. I'm also surprised that he is telling me all of this. He's treating me like I'm a friend, rather than just some kid.

"Yeah, I guess. But Kristin always reminded me to just try to stay in the present, if that makes any sense."

"Not really. How can you not think about stuff?"

"Well, you just try to live in the here and now, I guess. You don't let yourself go to those places in your mind where you worry about what he says or she says, or how you look, or what's going to happen ten years from now, or even tomorrow. You just live and be totally alive in the moment."

Now he sounds like Autumn Flower, Mom's spiritual advisor.

"The last book Kristin read was by a writer named Liz Gilbert. Some book about eating and praying. Anyway, Kristin liked to quote her whenever she saw me worrying too much about what was going to happen."

"What was the quote?" I ask.

"It's real simple: I will not harbor unhealthy thoughts anymore."

"That's it?"

"Yes, that's it. So whenever I start to feel sorry for myself, or sorry for Morgan because he lost his mom, I just say that over and over again. I will not harbor unhealthy thoughts anymore. And you know what? It usually works."

"Neat." I still don't really understand.

I think he can tell I'm not that interested because he turns up the volume and drives.

CHAPTER 50

When we get home, Ryan carries Morgan inside, and I pretend to act really tired. I yawn and stretch my arms.

"Long day," says Ryan, smiling.

"Yeah, long day. I think I'm going to turn in."

"I'll see you in the morning, Clementine. Good night."

Wow, this could possibly work out beautifully.

Morgan's asleep and it's 11:15. All I have to do is wait until midnight and sneak outside. I listen for Ryan. He doesn't turn on the TV; he goes to bed, too, which is perfect.

I wonder if I should climb out Morgan's window or risk sneaking out the front door. The window is already open and all I'll have to do is take the screen out. It isn't very high up and I know I can jump down easily. I decide the window route is my best bet. I sit quietly until the clock reads 11:50. I carefully use a pen to pry the screen from the window. Then I hop up onto the sill, turn around, and lower myself down. The window will have to stay open, but it's not raining or anything so I know it will be fine.

I quietly run to the front of the house and down the driveway, which isn't easy in my sparkly flip-flops. They keep making a flip-flop sound. Finally, I spot a big SUV with its parking lights on near the side of the road.

That must be them!

I run toward the truck, and the headlights come on. I hear laughing. Suddenly, I wonder if I should go ahead with this. I can still turn around and run back into the house. No, that would be such a baby thing to do. These guys seem so cool and grown up.

Brady's in the driver's seat. He buzzes the window down and whispers, "Clementine, get in!"

I run around to the passenger side; the door is already open for me. I'll be sitting up front with Brady.

Wow, it's like a date! Wait until Esther hears about this.

I hop in and shut the door, trying not to make a sound. Brady steps on the gas and we peel out, the tires spinning in the dirt. Everyone laughs and I pretend to, as well, but I'm worried that the noise could have woken up Ryan.

"So psyched you decided to come out with us!" I hear Sloane yell from the backseat.

"Me too!" I yell back.

"Do you want a smoke?" asks Brady.

"Um, no thanks. Not right now."

I've never smoked a cigarette before. They kind of gross me out. Brady lights one and buzzes the window down again.

"Where are we going?" I ask, wondering if there's a beach party happening or something like that.

"Sloane's dad has his boat parked down at the marina. It's a sweet ride. We thought we'd take the *Diversion* out, Diddy style. She's got two bedrooms and a kitchen."

"Wow," I say, trying to sound excited.

I wonder if he can tell that I'm suddenly really nervous. I have that feeling in my stomach again that this is all a really bad idea. I wonder how geeky it would be if I asked Brady to bring me back to Ryan and Morgan's house.

"Are you so glad you escaped out of that dump?" yells Blaine.

"Oh, it's not so bad," I reply. My hands are sweaty but I'm cold everywhere else.

"Give me a break. You're used to Beverly Hills. That place looks like it's going to fall down at any moment. And that kid. What's his name, Morgan? What a freak show!" Brady says, taking a puff of his cigarette.

Everyone in the back is laughing now. The truck is filled with smoke, and my eyes sting.

Hold it together. Hold it together. This is what high school kids do.

Before I can say anything more, we're already parking the truck and everyone's jumping out. Sloane finds me and puts her arm around my shoulders.

"Come on, you hang with me," she says with a smile.

That makes me feel better and more at ease. We walk arm in arm down a long dock. I wonder if we're at Ryan's dock, the one where he keeps his boat. But these are much bigger boats. They don't look like lobster boats.

"Here we are!" Sloane yells and points to a yacht to our right.

"Will your dad care that we're on the boat?" I ask, probably sounding like I'm seven.

"Um, what Daddy doesn't know won't hurt him. Get it?"

She sounds a little annoyed, so I make a mental note not to make comments like that anymore. I just need to act older.

We make our way onto the yacht and Sloane disappears down some steps. Lights come on from below. She reappears, dangling keys in her hand.

"Which one of you losers knows how to drive a boat?" she asks, looking straight at the boys.

One of them, whom I haven't been introduced to yet, grabs the keys and says, "That would be me, Captain Stud."

He disappears. Within minutes, I feel the vibration of the boat starting up. It's so dark, I wonder how he'll see where we're going. I also wonder where the life jackets are.

God, I am such a baby.

"Hey, let's go party down below," says Sloane.

Brady and I, plus the other girl, who says her name's Lauren, follow Sloane down the steps. It's like a real living room, with a big leather sectional, oversized chair, and flat-screen TV above the bar. It reminds me of my neighbor's boat in the Hamptons.

"Drinks are on the house!" yells Sloane as she heads to the refrigerator behind the wet bar.

"Sweet!" yells Lauren. "Vodka tonic for me!"

Oh, God. They're drinking. Of course, they're drinking.

"I'll just have a beer," says Brady, taking a seat on the couch.

"What would you like, Miss Calloway?" asks Sloane with a big smile.

"She'd like a dirty martini!" yells Lauren with a laugh.

"Dirty Martini" is one of Mom's songs. It was a huge hit.

"Oh, my God, that is so funny!" Sloane slurs. It seems like she's already drunk because she can barely stand up. "A dirty martini for Miss Calloway!"

"I'm actually all set," I say. I hope they'll just leave it at that.

"You can't be on a party boat and not have a drink," Sloane says, holding onto the wall so she won't fall.

"Really, I'm fine," I say.

The boat is moving now, and it seems like we're going pretty fast. I sit down next to Brady. So far, he seems the least drunk of the three.

"Wow, you're nothing like your mother, clearly," says Lauren, rolling her eyes at Sloane.

"Shut up, Lauren," says Brady.

"You shut up, Brady. All I'm saying is that her mother knows how to party. Is that such a bad thing?"

"I said I'm all set."

I turn my head and pretend to watch the television. Sloane sits down right next to me. She reeks of alcohol and her face is so close to mine.

"Tell me, so, like, how many boyfriends does your mom have right now?"

I can feel my face getting hotter and hotter. I'm not sure if I'll cry or just scream.

"None, actually," I say.

"Yeah, right, I heard she's dating, like, three Lakers," says Lauren, who's now halfway finished with her vodka drink.

"You guys are such witches," says Brady.

"Shut up, Brady. Why don't you go hang with the other boys? Or what, do you have the hots for Gray Calloway's daughter? You're sick, Brady. She's like a tween. How old are you, twelve?" Lauren is staring straight at me. I don't respond, but keep staring straight ahead.

"No, I just think you should leave her alone, that's all," he says. I totally agree.

My stomach turns because Brady decides to head upstairs with the other guys. I'm left with the two obnoxious drunk girls.

"So tell me," Sloane says, rubbing my shoulder, "like, does your mom just party all the time with other celebs?"

"Excuse me?" I ask. I'm done being polite.

"You know, like party and drink with all the other rock stars. I read it in *Celeb Weekly* magazine that she is really wild," Sloane says, trying to sound innocent.

Lauren is giggling so much, I think she'll spit out her drink.

"Well, you heard wrong," I reply.

"Oh, don't be so sensitive," Sloane slurs.

"Sensitive!" yells Lauren. "I love that song! Sing it with us, Clementine!"

"Sensitive" is another of Mom's hits. The two girls jump up, wrap their arms around each other, and sing it.

"I'm going to go get some air," I yell, but they're dancing and singing and ignore me as I make my way up the steps.

I find a quiet spot on a seat outside in the dark. We're traveling pretty fast, the motor is loud, and I'm comforted knowing that if I cry, no one will see my tears.

Suddenly, Brady's sitting next to me.

"Sorry about those two," he says, taking a puff of another cigarette. "They're totally wasted. Usually, they're not total bitches."

I just nod, pulling my knees up to my chest. The air is cold and I can barely see the lights from the island. I wish we'd just turn around and head back.

But we don't turn around. Instead, the boat comes to a stop in the middle of nowhere. The boys return to the deck where we're sitting, followed shortly by Lauren and Sloane, who can barely walk now. Someone turns on some music. It's so loud, you can barely hear anyone talk.

"This one's for Clementine!" yells Lauren at the stereo.

I know what she's going to play before the song comes on. It will be one of my mother's songs. Sure enough, "Dirty Martini" blares from the speakers.

"You like this, Clementine?" Lauren yells. Everyone's dancing now, except me and Brady, who just shakes his head and smokes his cigarette.

"Why are you such a downer? You're nothing like your mom! Get up and show us your moves!"

I tuck my knees up even closer to my chest and wish more than anything that I could just call someone. Call Mom, Marina, Ryan—even Morgan. Someone to get me out of this mess.

"Come on! Get up and dance!" Sloane takes my hand and pulls me up hard.

I almost fall but catch myself just in time.

"I really don't feel like dancing!" I yell.

"I don't care!" Sloane has both my hands now. "Stand up here!" She climbs up onto the seat where I had just been sitting. "This is like dancing on a bar!"

She pulls me up, and I suddenly realize that we are really close to the water.

"Let's just get down," I say, pulling her arms in.

"Yeah! Get down! Now you're talking!" She waves her arms, then suddenly wraps them around me and says, "I love you, Clementine."

Sloane has me in a big bear hug. Before I know it, she's falling. I struggle to push her away from me, but I'm locked in her embrace. The last thing I see is Brady jumping up to grab us, but he doesn't get to us in time.

I think I feel his hands on my ankles, but I'm not sure. When we hit the water, I lose my breath because it's so cold. Sloane is screaming, but I'm not.

I slip under, but then fight my way back to the surface. I come up gasping. The water is so cold, my hands burn and then go numb. The waves seem huge; I rise and fall with them, and they splash into my face as I try to keep my eyes on the boat. It looks like it's getting further and further away. I know I have to stay with it. It's so dark, they would never find me if I lost them. I try to remember what Coach from school told me to do in my swimming classes.

"Whatever you do, you stay calm," I can hear him say. "When you're out there, it's you against the water, and if you start panicking, you're done."

Don't panic. Don't panic. Don't panic.

I swim toward the boat, even though I can't feel my feet or even if they're kicking. I see the others on the boat frantically waving their arms and running around on deck. I hear someone yell, "Get the life ring!"

Though I'm swimming with all my might, the boat doesn't seem to be getting any closer. I hear Sloane crying and coughing. I want to help her, but I remember Coach always saying not to attempt a rescue if you don't have something to hold onto, like a rope or life preserver. She would just pull me under.

Just get to the boat.

My head is throbbing and I can hear my heart beating in my ears. I start to feel lightheaded. I keep hearing Coach say, "Swim, Clementine, swim! You can do it!"

I know if I stop, I'll never be able to start up again. I'm starting to feel numb all over.

I hear Sloane yelling, "Help me! I'm going to drown! Please help me!"

I start to cry, but I keep swimming. The boat seems closer now, but the waves keep splashing against me. I decide to take a big breath and swim under them. When I come up, I'm even closer.

"Clementine, grab this!" It's Brady. He has a life preserver that he's tied onto the boat somehow.

"No!" I scream. "Throw it to Sloane! I can hold onto the boat! She's going to drown!"

Brady dashes to the back of the boat and I watch him throw the preserver.

"Oh, God!" he yells.

He must have missed. He pulls the preserver back on board and I watch him throw it again.

"Sloane, swim to it!" he yells.

"I can't!" she sobs.

"You have to or you'll die!" he yells back.

A few seconds go by and I finally make my way to the boat. I put my hand on the side of it. It's bobbing up and down so much, I think it might crush me. I move away and follow along the side to the back of the boat. I know there has to be something here for me to hold onto.

I find a small hook about the size of my hand. I grab onto it and hold on as best as I can. It lifts me up and down as the boat bobs in the rough water. My hand shakes and I know I can't hold on for very long. I can barely feel my fingers.

Oh Grandpa, I'm in big trouble. I really need you. Please don't let me die. Mom needs me. I'm sorry I've been so awful. Please let me live and I'll be better. I'll stop worrying so much, just like Ryan said. I'll be a better person. Please Grandpa, give me strength.

I'm crying again. Sobbing, actually. As I sob, I breathe in a wave of water. It burns my throat.

My hand is going to let go. I can't hold on. I can't hold on. Please, Grandpa. Help me hold on.

Suddenly, a gigantic light shines on me.

"Clementine! Hold on!"

Oh, my God! Ryan!

He's calling from behind me. I hear a loud splash; within seconds, I feel his arms around me.

"I got you, Clementine," he pants. "I got you."

CHAPTER 51

I don't remember much about the ride back to shore, but I have some flashbacks of being in the ambulance with Morgan and Ryan sitting next to me. One EMT is busy covering me in blankets while the other is phoning ahead to the hospital. I hear him say something about hypothermia.

I try to make eye contact with Ryan. I want to tell him how sorry I am. I feel a hand on my hand and realize it's Morgan's.

"She's so cold," I hear him whisper.

"She's going to be OK," Ryan replies.

There's an oxygen mask over my face so I can't talk. But I turn my hand around so I can hold Morgan's. He smiles at me.

I must have fallen asleep, because the next thing I remember is waking up in a hospital room. Ryan's sitting next to me and jumps up when I open my eyes. Morgan is curled up in a chair, sleeping.

"Clementine, you're awake. How do you feel?" Ryan looks so scared.

"I'm OK. Where's Sloane? Is she OK?"

"She's OK. Some hypothermia like you, and pretty dehydrated from the liquor, but she's going to be OK."

"Ryan—" I begin.

"It's OK," he says and pats my hand.

"No, it's not."

I try to sit up, but I feel so tired. And my hands and legs feel all prickly.

"Clementine, you need rest," Ryan says.

"No Ryan, I need to say something."

I sit up as best I can. "I'm so sorry for sneaking out. It was so stupid. But mostly, I'm sorry for being awful for the past four days. I'm usually not a mean person."

"It's OK, Clementine. You were just being stupid. Kids do that sometimes. And as far as how you've been acting, well, I think that's really between you and that boy sleeping right over there. He was so worried about you.

"You know, since his mom died, he's been amazing. Hardly ever complains. He works hard, in school and with me. He cleans the house, helps me with cooking, and never asks for anything, not even new clothes. Now, I know he's a little different, but you know what? I'm glad. I'm glad that he skips around and whistles. And I'm glad that he wears a Mickey Mouse T-shirt because he thinks it will remind you of home. That just tells me what an amazing kid he is.

"He lives in the moment. He doesn't worry much about what he thinks or she thinks. He just lives each moment and appreciates life. Probably got that from his mom. Now I suggest that when this is all over, you give him a chance. He's sure been excited about getting to know you, Clementine. I can't remember the last time he's been that excited."

Tears are rolling down my face again, and I wipe them away.

"I know," I sob.

And I do know. I want to be more like Morgan. I know I have to stop worrying about things in the future, like how much I worried about that stupid dance. It suddenly dawns on me—if you're so busy worrying about the future, you miss out on the here and now.

Ryan puts his hand on my head.

"You're a good kid, Clementine," he says. "You've just got a lot to deal with. More than most kids, I guess. You're going to figure this all out, and be better for it."

I nod and look over at Morgan, who now has drool seeping down the side of his face.

"Clementine, how'd your mom come up with that name, anyway?" Ryan asks, sitting down and putting his arm around Morgan.

"She craved them when she was pregnant," I say. "I guess my grandfather bought out a whole grocery store full of them one week."

"Well, then, I guess it's a good think she didn't crave flounder." He smiles and rubs Morgan's head. I laugh.

"Ryan, how'd you find me?" I ask.

I'm tired now, but I can't stop thinking how grateful I am that he found me, floating in the middle of the Atlantic like that.

"Didn't Miss Lyle tell you? Everyone knows everyone on Chebeague. You can't get away with anything. Remember Wyatt, the deckhand from the ferry? He was down at the marina, closing everything up for the night. He thought he recognized you from your ferry ride out here. Called me right away."

"Wow, I'll have to thank him," I say, rolling over on my side. "Oh, and Ryan?"

"Yeah, Clem?"

"We really need to do something about the Mickey Mouse T-shirt."

He laughs. "I know. It's awful, isn't it?"

I roll over smiling and go back to sleep, Morgan at my side.

CHAPTER 52

The sun beams through the window when I wake up the next morning at Maine Medical Center. I feel much better, and the prickly feeling in my hands and toes is gone. I sit up and wonder if I can make it to the bathroom.

That's when I see her—and I think I'm dreaming. She's curled up in the chair that Morgan had been sleeping in. I feel tears welling up in my eyes again. She's wearing jeans, a long-sleeved T-shirt, and her tortoiseshell glasses. I can smell her Coco Chanel perfume.

"Mommy," I whisper. I'm not sure how she hears me, but she wakes up and smiles.

"Baby!" She rushes over to me and I think she's going to jump in my bed. She's crying. "Please don't do that to me again. I thought I lost you!"

She's holding on to me tightly; I hold on to her just as hard.

"I'm so sorry, Mommy," I whisper into her shoulder.

"I know you are, baby, I know you are," she says, still crying.

She sits back and wipes her eyes. "You know what?" she begins. "This can be a big lesson for both of us. How about you not go on boats with strange teenagers, and I'll be there for my daughter when she needs me?"

"That sounds really good," I say, laughing a little.

She hops into bed next to me, and I put my head on her shoulder. We talk about all that's happened. I tell her how it made me so mad when those kids were talking about her on the boat. She just shakes her head and strokes my hair. Then she tells me a little more about the stupid things she's done that have almost killed her. By the end of it, we're both laughing so hard, we're crying.

My mom gives me a choice. I can fly back with her to New York, or I can stay for the remainder of my time in Maine. It's not a hard decision. I know immediately what I'll do.

"I want to stay, Mom," I say. She's not surprised.

"Do you want me to stay with you?" she asks.

"What, and cancel the rest of your tour? That's crazy. I need to do this on my own."

"Do you want me to fly Marina and Jesus-Marco out to stay with you?"

We both laugh again, picturing Jesus-Marco terrorizing the island of Chebeague.

"I'm proud of you," she says. "You're braver than I am. I think I'd run for the hills if I were you."

"No, you wouldn't. And by the way, I'm proud of you too."

"For what?" she asks, surprised.

"I heard that you're giving half the money from your concerts to UNICEF."

"Well, yes. I wish I could do more, but someone has to keep the lights on in our house. Oh, and buy Marina a new car."

"You did?"

"Absolutely. That thing was a death box."

We both laugh, thinking about it. I think of how excited Marina must have been when she got her new car.

"Yeah, UNICEF is doing some amazing work," Mom says. "You and I should both get more involved with it when the tour is over and you're back from Maine."

"That would be great."

"One of my friends works for UNICEF, and she just adopted the most adorable baby girl from Africa."

"Wow," I say. "That's great."

"It got me thinking. You and I have so much room in that big house of ours. And we have so much love to give. What would you think about doing something like that?"

"Are you insane? Mom, you can barely take care of me, let alone an African baby!"

She laughs and snuggles closer to me. "I know, I know. It's crazy. But I was just thinking what an amazing big sister you'd be. And I am so done with touring. I still want to record and write. And I'd really love to produce and write for some of these young, up-and-coming chicks. I'd take them under my wing, keep them out of trouble."

"You'd be good at that," I said. "And you'd be good at being a mom again, too."

"I love you, Clem."

"I love you, too," I answer. "Now, what would we name this baby?"

"Hmm, it would have to go nicely with Clementine."

"Mom, we're not giving her a fruit name. Or a vegetable, or anything weird, for that matter."

"OK, well, what would you name her?"

"I like the name Kristin."

"That's really pretty. Kristin."

CHAPTER 53

It's 10 a.m., and we're waiting for the doctor to sign the discharge papers so I can leave. Mom's on the phone with Hali when Morgan and Ryan appear in my doorway. Morgan's holding flowers wrapped at the bottom with tinfoil. They look like he's just picked them. They're beautiful—purples and blues, my favorite. They both look tired, and Ryan's clutching a big cup of coffee.

"How you feeling, Clem? You ready to bust out of here?" Ryan asks.

"Absolutely. I'm feeling great. Thanks again for rescuing me," I say, slipping on my shoes.

"Rumor has it that if it wasn't for you, that girl Sloane might not have made it," Morgan says, handing me the flowers.

"Thanks, they're beautiful. And about that—well, anyone else would've done the same thing."

Mom's off the phone and gives Morgan and Ryan big hugs.

"Boy, you two," she says with a smile, "I owe you big time."

"Nonsense." Ryan shakes his head. "Actually, you know what you can do? You can stay another night. Morgan and I are going to go home and get ready for the biggest and best lobster bake you've ever seen."

"Well, I suppose I could still have laryngitis for one more day before I head back," Mom says, winking at me. Hali had reported to the media that Mom's vocal cords were strained, and she therefore had to take a little time off from her shows. Fans' tickets would be fully refunded. If the media had gotten wind that there was some kind of accident, they would have followed her like a hawk. Instead, she was able to sneak away with only Rocco the bodyguard.

Rocco peeks his big, bald head in the door. He's not wearing his sunglasses, and he gives me a wink. I smile back.

"Well, that is an offer I can't refuse," Mom says, sitting on the bed and taking my hand in hers. "I have never been to a real Maine lobster bake."

"Really?" asks Morgan, his eyes wide.

Before she can answer, I hear a soft knock on the door. I turn to see Georgia standing there, holding a book in her hands. Her hair is in braids again, and she's dressed up in a pink skirt with purple flowers on it and a white T-shirt.

"Hi, Clementine. I just wanted to come and see how you were doing. I'm so sorry about the accident," she says, still standing in the doorway.

"Come in, come in," I say, feeling terrible for the way I've treated her, judged her.

"Georgia, this is my mom, Gray."

"Hi, Miss Calloway, pleased to meet you," Georgia says, holding out her hand to Mom.

"So nice to meet you," Mom says. "Gosh, you're so pretty! And, please, call me Gray."

Georgia beams and blushes.

"I brought you this, Clementine. I want you to have it. I think you'll like it."

Georgia holds out a book wrapped with a blue ribbon.

"*A Collection of Longfellow's Poetry,*" I read aloud. "Thank you so much, Georgia."

"You're welcome," she says.

We all chat for about twenty minutes, telling stories like how I nearly died jumping off the rope swing. Mom's laughing like I haven't seen her laugh in a long time, her hand on mine all the while.

Someone else knocks on the door, and, with a big smile on her face, Miss Lyle hobbles in on her crutches.

"Well, Miss Clementine," she says, "I was really hoping that just one of us would have to make a visit to Maine Med this week. How about we not tell Mr. Consuelos about this one, OK?"

I laugh and get up to hug her. "That's a deal," I say and wrap my arms around her.

She sits for a while and we all sign her cast. She looks beautiful; something about being home in Maine seems to suit her. She looks so relaxed, her cheeks rosy from the sun.

I never see Sloane or any of the others again while I'm here.

And that's fine with me.

CHAPTER 54

Mom's staying at the Inn for the night, and she's gone back there with Rocco to freshen up before the lobster bake. Ryan has invited a lot of people, including Miss Lyle and her family, Georgia and her family, Leon, some neighbors, and even Bud Sanders. I ask Ryan if Bud will bring his guitar.

"That man doesn't go anywhere without his guitar," Ryan says as he loads folding chairs into the back of the truck. We're going to have the lobster bake on the beach, so there's a lot to pack.

Morgan and I help carry two folding metal tables from the garage. We need to leave extra time, because we'll also need to dig a big pit, where we'll cook the lobsters, potatoes, corn, and clams. I'm getting hungry just thinking about it.

We stop at the market and buy lots of potatoes, onions, butter, sodas, water, and—of course—whoopie pies. I can't wait for Mom to try one.

When we get to the beach, we go to work immediately. The sun is still warm on our backs as we dig and dig the massive hole in the sand, about four feet deep and six feet wide. Morgan and I line the bottom with large stones and the sides with smaller ones. Morgan tells me the more stones we use, the hotter the pit will be. Then Ryan sends Morgan and me to scrub the potatoes in the ocean. It's hard work, having a lobster bake, but there's no place I'd rather be.

"You seem different, Clementine," says Morgan as he rinses a potato. "Happier."

"I guess I am," I say. "Thinking that you're going to die can kind of change your perspective on things, you know?"

"Or watching someone you love get really sick," he says, watching a wave crash.

"Yeah, I can't even imagine. Morgan, that must have been horrible."

"It just kind of makes you decide right then and there not to worry about those little things, like who says what about you. And that voice, you know that one that tells you that the person you like may not like you back or that your clothes aren't as nice as the person who sits behind you in math class? Well, you just kind of learn to turn that voice off, or at least turn the volume down a few notches."

"Yeah, I need to practice doing that."

We're silent for a few seconds.

"Clementine, are you glad you're here, or do you think you want to go back when your mom leaves?"

"I want to stay, if that's OK with you," I say. After all, I have been a horrible guest, and I wouldn't be surprised if he wants me to leave.

"Of course I'd love you to stay. We'll start over. How about that?"

"That would be great. And Morgan—"

"You don't need to say anything," he says, looking embarrassed.

"I'm sorry," I say, putting my hand on his.

He smiles and holds up his other hand. There's seaweed hanging off his wrist. He extends his hand to shake. "Hi, I'm Morgan."

Smiling, I put my hand out and take his. "Hi, I'm Clementine."

And for a second—. No, no way. This is Morgan. Well, for a second, I think—just for a second—I feel butterflies in my stomach.

He smiles and pushes a curl off his forehead.

"Race you to the pier!" he says with a big grin.

I take off running, and laughing, and don't look back once.

CHAPTER 55

The lobster bake is more fun than I could ever have imagined. Mom and Rocco actually show up early to see if we need any help. She has her hair in a ponytail, and she's wearing a cream wool sweater and jeans. Amazingly, I think she looks like a New Englander, not the LA celebrity mom I'm used to seeing.

I don't think I've ever eaten so much. The lobsters are huge, and Ryan shows us precisely how to crack the shells and eat the delicious meat. And when I say huge, it's an understatement. Maine lobsters are gigantic, about the size of my forearm. Not at all like the ones I've eaten in California. There are also clams dipped in melted butter and fresh corn on the cob. And Mom absolutely loves the whoopie pie.

"Wouldn't a dozen whoopie pies be the most fabulous Christmas gift to give this year?" she asks, biting into one.

Miss Lyle arrives with her parents, and Skip and Ryan hit it off really well. They talk for at least an hour.

Then Bud Sanders strolls in with his guitar, and immediately everyone sits in front of him like he's a storyteller. I join Georgia and Morgan right up front. I whisper to Georgia how much I love my Longfellow book, and I tell her that my favorite poem is "The Children's Hour."

"That's a great one," she agrees.

Instead of singing, Bud flattens his hand on the guitar and talks. "Normally, I'm content to sing alone, but I hear we got ourselves a real singer in the house tonight, and, boy, I'd be flattered if she joined me up here. Gray?"

Mom's standing in the back of the group, talking to Miss White, the teacher Ryan supposedly has a crush on.

Mom looks at Bud, smiles, and nods. She makes her way to the front and sits down beside him. He points to an extra guitar and she grabs it and puts it around her neck.

"Do you happen to know 'Life in a Northern Town,' Miss Calloway?"

"Why, yes I do Mr. Sanders," she says. She looks at me and winks.

"Well then, take it away," he says and gives her a nod.

Bud strums and Mom begins to sing. Everyone sways back and forth. I feel so proud. Even though I've heard her sing in front of thousands of people, tonight she just sounds more beautiful than ever.

Later, Bud sings songs I actually recognize. I smile at Skip when he plays a Lyle Lovett song. Ryan, Morgan, Mom, and everyone create a dance floor right on the sand under the Maine stars. And we dance the night away. I can't remember the last time I had that much fun.

It's a perfect night, and I have to say that, for the first time in a long time, I am really, truly happy.

CHAPTER 56

Mom's leaving on the morning ferry, so she and Rocco stop by Ryan and Morgan's house to say good-bye at 9 a.m. She looks more LA now, with her long black dress and black sunglasses.

"I'm going to miss you, Clem," she says, giving me a big hug.

"I'll miss you, too, Mom, but we've only got, like, a week left until I see you again," I remind her.

We've decided that, at the end of my stay in Maine, I'll go to New York. Mom and I will maybe see a Broadway show and also get my hair fixed, then fly back to California together. That sounds much better than flying again with Leon.

"So Rocco is going to take you to Boston," Mom says. "I think you guys will take a train from Portland, Maine to Boston. From there, I'll send a jet for you, and we'll meet up in New York, OK?"

"That's fine," I say.

"Hey Clem, do you need anything else before I go? Do you need any money or anything?"

"No, but if you could do me one favor, I'd really appreciate it."

"Sure, name it."

I hold out Roy Rudebaker's business card, the exit-sign salesman who sat next to me on the plane. "Could you have Hali send him a ticket to your New York show? He's a big fan. Maybe even a backstage pass?"

She looks at the card, puzzled. "Who the heck is Roy Rudebaker?"

"He's just a nice man I met on the plane ride to Maine."

"No problem. I'll have Hali call him and tell him that there will be a ticket at the box office for him. Actually, I can do better than that. Maybe I'll call Roy myself and tell him I'm sending a limo to bring him to the show."

I smile and hug her, picturing how happy Roy will be when she calls him.

Rocco leans his big, bald head in the door, looks straight at me, and says, "No more monkey business out of you, you hear me?"

I laugh and nod. Mom gives Ryan and Morgan a hug, too, and within minutes, they're gone.

"So what'll it be today, Miss Clementine? Blueberry pancakes?" Ryan asks, putting a dish towel over his shoulder.

"Actually, I was thinking I'd cook for you boys. Eggs a la Clementine," I say, smiling.

"Wow, that sounds great. I think I'll take my coffee, then, and go sit outside while you cook. This is a real treat." Ryan picks up the newspaper and heads to the porch.

"Do you want some help?" asks Morgan.

"Sure," I say. "We'll need to chop some green peppers, tomatoes, and onions. Can you do that?"

"Absolutely," he replies.

I laugh because Morgan's already wearing a pink apron with ruffles.

After breakfast, Ryan leans back and says, "Well, Clementine, if I'd known you could cook like that, I wouldn't have been slaving away in the kitchen for the past five days."

I laugh and reply, "They were just eggs."

But they had come out really good. At home, they call it a California scramble. Eggs, cheese, onion, peppers. Marina is really good at making them.

"So what are you guys going to do today?" Ryan asks.

"What do you want to do, Clementine?" Morgan says.

"I'd like to tackle that rope swing, if you're up for it," I say determinedly.

Morgan smiles. "Sounds great. Should I call Georgia?"

"Definitely," I reply.

CHAPTER 57

Even though I try not to think about returning to Los Angeles, my time in Maine flies by anyway. But we have so much fun. I dominate the rope swing, and even master a trick that Georgia has yet to try—a swing-out backward dive.

We take lots of hikes through the woods and go out at least five times on Ryan's boat. One day, we even persuade him to ask Miss White to join us, which she does. The two of them chat away all day, and I can tell they really like each other. For a moment, I kind of wish that he and Mom could have gotten to know each other, but then I laugh, thinking of Mom as a lobsterman's wife. It would never work. And picturing Ryan in Los Angeles is even funnier.

We have lots of dance parties in Morgan's room with Georgia. By dance party, I mean we just play his boom box really loud and dance and sing. Ryan peeks in and just shakes his head.

On my last night, we eat dinner out on the porch. Ryan lit some candles, and once again, we're feasting on lobster.

"You're going back to California sick of lobster, I bet," says Morgan, cracking open a shell.

"How could anyone get sick of lobster?" I ask, cracking a tail. I'm a real pro now and know exactly how to eat a lobster the correct way. I like to take out all the meat first, put it in the butter, and then eat it all at once.

"Morgan, why don't you give it to her now?" asks Ryan.

"OK, Dad, I will. Clementine, we picked out a little something for you. Something to help you remember us." Morgan hands me a small white box.

"I won't need help remembering you guys," I say, taking the box from Morgan's hand.

I open it and carefully pull out a beautiful necklace. It's a soapstone pendant shaped like a turtle, with dark blue numbers and letters painted on it.

"I love it," I say. "Thank you so much."

"Well, do you know what it is?"

"I know it's a turtle. But I'm not sure about the letters and numbers," I respond curiously.

"It's our island, Clem," Ryan says. "The island of Chebeauge is actually shaped like a turtle. And 43N44, 70W07, those are the coordinates of Chebeague."

"Oh, you mean like the latitude and longitude?" I ask.

"Yes, exactly," Ryan says. "Explorers, sailors, lobstermen, daughters of rock stars—we all use coordinates to find our way. So when you need to check your bearings, just think of those of us on the island who care about you. It will remind you to stay strong when you need to, just like you did that night in the Atlantic. And Clementine, try not to be in a big rush to grow up, you know what I mean?"

"And it will also remind you of how to get back here," Morgan chimes in. "Anytime you want to come back."

I smile. Part of me wishes that I could stay here forever, where people wouldn't look twice if I wanted to skip all the way to the beach with Morgan. And I laugh, thinking how stupid those cutlets were, and the spray tan, for that matter. I also realize that although my home is not really like a normal home, and that my mom is never going to be like most other moms, I'm okay. I know that I'm pretty lucky. I have all these people that love me- Mom, Marina, Esther, Rocco, Henry, Ryan, Morgan, Georgia, Miss Lyle, and even Jesus Marco. And I look up at the stars which are so beautiful and clear here in Maine, and I silently say, "Thank you."

CHAPTER 58

Early the next morning, we are heading down the hill in Ryan's truck to the ferry. I wear my new necklace and a pair of L.L. Bean boots that Morgan says are too small for him. I think they look great with my white denim mini-skirt and plaid shirt. The sky is bright blue as we board the ferry, and Wyatt greets us at the door. He must recognize me because he asks how my stay was.

"It was amazing," I say. "And I really owe you a huge thank you. You kind of saved my life by calling Ryan that night."

"Hey, no worries. That's what we Mainers do. We look out for each other."

"Yeah, I heard that," I reply with a smile.

We sit on top of the ferry, and I take lots of pictures. I want to remember everything. How the Inn looks from the water, how the little houses dot the shoreline.

Morgan and I really don't talk much on the ferry or the bus. I think we're both feeling sad about the good-byes we'll have to say in the next hour. On the bus ride, I gaze out the window, remembering this same ride with Miss Lyle's parents. So much has changed.

Before I know it, the bus is pulling into the train station. I see Rocco, standing out like a sore thumb. Dressed in black from head to toe, with his black sunglasses, he looks more like a movie villain than a bodyguard. He waves to us as we step down from the bus.

Ryan gives me a hug. "Well, this is it, Clementine. I hope you'll come back. Maybe next summer, even?"

"That would be great," I say.

"Make sure you write," says Morgan.

"I will," I reply, giving him a big hug. "Maybe next time, you can come visit me." I smile at the thought of Morgan in Los Angeles.

"I'd like that," he says.

Rocco points toward the train. "Time to go, Clem," he says.

I know that if I say much more, I'll cry, and I don't want to do that. I give Ryan and Morgan one last smile, pick up my bag, and follow Rocco onto the train. I look out the window. I see Ryan put his arm around Morgan's shoulder and rub it.

Morgan and I exchange smiles as I lean back against my seat. I press my hand to the window, and he puts his hand in the air.

And then I hear the train's engine start up.

"You ready, kiddo?" asks Rocco.

"Ready," I reply. And I really am.

Then I lean back and smile.

43N44,70W07

10259012R00188

Made in the USA
Charleston, SC
20 November 2011